Deadly Treasure

Deadly Treasure

A Diana Hunter Thriller

Joan Francis

Lobathian Publishers

PARTNERS IN CRIME

My thanks to my Palmdale Partners in Crime, for their reading, editing, critiquing and encouragement in bringing this book to completion. Find all of the Partners In Crime Writers and our books at: http://www.kevinburtonsmith.com/partners_in_crime.html

MINOAN GAMES

In this story all of the art work that Diana must find was originally a product of my imagination. However I was delighted to find that a modern day artist has created a beautiful sculpture that brings one of those pieces to life. I am thrilled that he has allowed me to use a photo image of his sculpture on the cover of this book.

The artist is Michel Paul Richard and his sculpture is titled, *Minoan Games*. Of his sculpture he writes:

The inspiration for my sculpture Minoan Games came from a visit to the island of Crete in 1985. While there my wife Peggy and I visited the Palace of Minos and were struck by a fresco depicting an acrobat balanced on the back of a charging bull. He is in an inverted position with hands grasping its flanks. A spotter stands behind the bull with arms outstretched towards the acrobat, while another assistant stands in front of the bull grasping its horns. As Arthur Evans points out in his book Palace of Minos, this depiction is purely iconic, and I decided to go with a more realistic interpretation with a female acrobat vaulting over the horns in a front handspring. My bronze sculpture was completed in 1993.

You can find more about the artist, Michel Paul Richard and his art work at his web site: www.michelpaulrichard.com

CHAPTER ONE

Under half closed eyelids I looked surreptitiously through the veil of my hat to see how many people I could identify. I wasn't crying. I had gotten control of that before the service. In fact I had not only finished crying, I had suppressed all emotion, and become cold and analytical. That's always been my way of coping.

The family box was positioned in the front of the chapel looking outward at the congregation. Yes, there was a smoked glass window, supposedly providing privacy for the grieving family, but as I sat there alone, the only surviving family member, I felt quite exposed. I was thankful for my hat's veil, an additional shield between my emotions and the world.

The number of people who had found their way to Bluff Beach, California, on very short notice to attend my father's funeral was a shock. He had never lived in Bluff Beach, and as far as I knew he had as few close friends as I had. As an exploratory mining engineer, he was seldom in one place long enough to make friends, and throughout my childhood, we two had tramped around the world together, in a solitary vagabond life.

When I arranged for a quiet evening service, I thought the only attendees would be my long time friend Jenny and her family, my friend and mentor, Sam Dehany, and me. Instead, thirty or forty people sat in somber silence in the Veterans Chapel in Long Beach as the Chaplain dutifully praised my father's life using information I had supplied to him.

As I studied the attendees, I heard little the Chaplain said. I recognized a few as men who had been in mining with Dad over the years. But those men I had known in far away parts of the world. How had they heard about his death? Why had they shown up and from where? Hell, for that matter who had completed the necessary paperwork and sent a sealed coffin to be buried here in California? Most importantly, where and how had Dad died? He had been in good health and no explanation of his death had accompanied his mysteriously shipped coffin. It had arrived at the Long Beach Veterans Administration complex with nothing but the necessary legal documents which listed me as next of kin and had provided my last known address here in Bluff Beach.

There was a main door at the back of the chapel and a side exit to my right. As the Chaplain's comments drew to a close, I considered leaving quickly by the side door to avoid the dreaded process of standing and accepting condolences from all present. However my curiosity about who they were and how they knew my dad argued for staying and attending the reception that was set up in the next room. Several of them didn't look like Dad's mining friends.

I was especially curious about a lovely older woman, just about Dad's age. She drew my attention the minute she came into the chapel because she, Jenny, and I were the only women present. She was about five feet, two inches tall, had short curly hair, sparkling dark eyes and a round face with small features that reminded me of Claudette Colbert. She wore a nice wool suit in muted shades of lavender, and the lapel was accented with a flower made of the same fabric as the suit. Her style looked more New York or London than Bluff Beach. She was of medium build. Her dark brown hair laced with grey was well groomed and toped with a brown hat. She wore solid brown shoes with a broad, inch and a half heel. Though built for a mature walking stride, they were still quite stylish. The only flaw in her appearance was the feather in her hat. It had been broken and lay lopsided on the hat. My best guess was that she was in a chapter of his life that Dad had failed to mention.

My cell phone vibrated in my suit pocket. I would have ignored it but at the exact moment it began to vibrate, the lady I was looking at jumped as if startled and looked down at her suit coat pocket. Trying to be inconspicuous she slipped a gloved hand into her pocket and discreetly pulled out a cell phone. Her response then was anything but discreet. Her mouth dropped open and she covered it with her free hand as if to prevent a cry. She pressed the phone to her chest and looked around the room. Then carefully she pulled the phone down below the back of the pew in front of her and read her message. She became visibly pale and looked directly at me.

My cell phone continued to vibrate insistently. After seeing the look on the woman's face, I pulled my cell and held it behind the memorial program of my father's service. Staring up at me from the screen was my father's picture and the following message: "Chick, my friend Abbie needs a new hat. Please go with her immediately. Keep her safe. She doesn't fly. You girls will have to go by ship. Tickets and details attached. Town car is waiting just out the side entrance."

I looked back at the woman I assumed must be Abbie. We stared at each other in disbelief.

What the hell was going on? I was sitting at my father's funeral and getting messages from him. And this was not a seance message from beyond the grave. This was a frigging text message that was definitely coming from my Dad's cell phone.

My first thought was that someone was pulling a terribly cruel hoax. I looked around the chapel to see if I could spot anyone with a cell phone. I saw no one. Besides, my analytical side was providing second thoughts about the message.

There were two things in that message that suggested it might really be coming from my father. He was the only one in the world who called me Chick. He used to joke that he was an old rooster with only one baby chick. Of course, some of his old mining buddies might have heard him call me that, but I was quite sure that the "new hat" reference would have significance only to me and Dad.

After Mom died, Dad kept me with him rather than sticking me in a boarding school. But his job meant that we moved very frequently. When Dad knew it was time to uproot me again, he would say, "Well, Chick, I guess it's time to buy a new hat." He would follow that with a geographical game of twenty questions until I guessed where we were headed. Then we would go buy a hat that fit the climate or the clothing style of our next destination. That was Dad's way of making the move be about a new adventure rather than about parting from current friends.

I looked back up at Abbie. Then in unison, our eyes were drawn to the closed coffin.

The phone began to vibrate again. Abbie and I looked down at our phones simultaneously. The message on mine read: "DO NOT OPEN THE COFFIN, DO NOT HESITATE. LEAVE NOW!"

Abbie was on her feet and heading for the side door before I had time to evaluate the message. I had no choice but to follow her.

CHAPTER TWO

Searching the parking lot in the twilight, I spotted Abbie a few feet away and just about to step into a gleaming black Town Car. I ran to her and grabbed her arm. "Abbie, wait, don't you think we should check out these messages before we hop into some strange car."

She hesitated a moment, looked over her shoulder at the driver who was holding the car door open. Then she held up her phone to show me the latest message. It read, "Bunnie, don't talk in front of the driver."

My latest message said: "Chick, tell the driver to take you to the San Pedro passenger terminal, but don't give him any extra information. Get it?"

Bunnie and Chick? Whoever was texting us knew Dad's nickname for me and I assumed Bunnie must be what Dad called Abbie. Our mystery texter also seemed to know mine and Dad's little code. To test that I answered, "Got it."

He responded, "Good."

"Get it, got it, good." There were only two people in the world who used that old Danny Kaye bit with me, Jenny and my Dad.

Powerful confused emotions welled up inside of me, threatening to break through the calm I was using to hold myself together. "Chick, Bunnie, new hat, get it, got it, good." After all the pain of loss, I was almost certain those texts had to be coming from my Dad. He had to be alive? Was it just that I wanted to believe he was alive. Had someone just researched the ultimate con? What the hell was going on?

My friend, Jenny appeared from behind me and grabbed my arm as I had grabbed Abbie's. "Diana, what's wrong? The reception is right next door. Where are you going?"

Next, Sam opened the side door of the chapel and stood watching us. I had no answers for the questions Jenny and Sam would ask. Abbie had climbed into the car and was giving me a pleading look to get in. I looked back at Jenny and said the first thing that occurred to me. "I guess I'm going to go buy a new hat."

"What? Are you all right?"

I couldn't blame her for looking at me as if I were nuts. It was a silly thing to say.

"Look, Jenny, I can't explain now, but I have to go. Please make my apologies and tell everyone I was too upset to stay for the reception. I'll call you and Sam when I can. And, Jenny, please make sure everyone signs the guest book and leaves an address."

I climbed into the Town Car, and as the driver shut the door I realized that Sam had not tried to walk over to the car or stop me. He seemed to be watching to make sure I got to the car all right. He rested one arm across the chapel door as if blocking it so no one else could follow us out. What did Sam know that I didn't? What was he hiding from me *this time*. As the driver put our car in gear I saw Sam's head whip around. He was looking at two men getting into a black Buick in the front parking lot. They were short and very slender and their clothes looked more European than American. I couldn't see their faces. They started up the Buick and drove toward us but were stopped by a low barricade that separated the two lots. I could see their faces then and the disgruntled look when they realized they could not drive through. They could almost be brothers, slender bony faces, dark eyes, sharp check bones, prominent noses, and olive skin. The driver whipped the car around and spitting gravel from its tires, drove rapidly up the long lot past construction barriers to find an exit.

"Go driver," I said.

"Ah, where would you ladies like me to go?"

"Weren't you given instructions?"

"Yes, Ma'am, but just to pick you up here and take you wherever you needed to go."

"Ok, for now just drive up PCH. We will give you directions as we go."

As we left by the side entrance, I watched the Buick as it pulled out of the front parking lot and raced around to take up a spot several cars behind us. While I watched the Buick, Abbie opened emails with tickets and timetables and tried to show them to me without talking. I waved her off.

My thoughts were going in too many directions at once. Sam had called me in North Carolina to tell me of a message that had come in on my old Bluff Beach phone number. The message said simply that my father was dead and his body was being shipped to the Veterans' Hospital complex in Long Beach because it was close to the last known residence of his only family, me. I had spent the days since trying to accept that my father was really dead. The last time I had heard from him he had been checking out a barite mine in Kazakstan and he was just fine.

I had called every source and checked every lead I could think of to find out what had happened to him. Now, through the magic of a cell phone, he seemed to be sending me messages from beyond the grave. Had he put me through this pain for nothing? No, he would never be that cruel. If he was sending these messages he was in one hell of a lot of trouble

I turned my thoughts to something I could deal with, something I could analyze and understand. The Buick was pacing us a few cars back. "Driver, take the next right, go three blocks, then take a left and in two more blocks another right."

He followed my instructions, making careful, legal turns, using his signal and driving like a sixteen-year-old on his first driving test. The Buick followed with no difficulty and left no doubt that we were being tailed. They stayed too far back for me to get their plate, but the look I got of their faces confirmed they had attended Dad's service. I am cursed with very poor visual memory, a bad trait for a private investigator. In order to save the memory of those faces, I had to change what I saw into words and remember the words because the visual memory was already fading.

"Driver, stay in the right lane but in the next block watch for an opening to take a fast sharp left across traffic and up onto the 405 freeway. Don't use your signal."

He stopped for a light and looked back at me. I really looked at him for the first time. He was young and good looking with blond hair, brown eyes, and long lashes. The look he gave me was incredulous. "A sharp left across traffic from the right lane. You want me to lose my license?"

"No, I want you try to lose our tail. Check them out in the mirror. Two guys in a black Buick, four cars back. Try to time that left turn at the very end of the light so they are blocked by cross traffic and give us a head start down the freeway."

He broke into a smile. "No shi . . . Er, no kidding? Somebody's tailing us?"

"Yeah, they've been behind us every turn from the chapel." Though it would make my request no more legal, I pulled out my PI license and showed it to him. "I'm a licensed private investigator and I have to get this woman to safety. I need your help."

He considered the license, then me, then Abbie. "Cool," he said. He turned eyes front, pulled his cap down tight and when the light changed, he moved slowly down the street timing his arrival at the next light perfectly. When the left lane was clear of cars and the light was long into the yellow, he stomped the gas, made a quick left through the intersection just a second before the cross traffic got their green light and filled the street, effectively blocking the Buick. He floored the gas peddle as he raced up the freeway on-ramp.

"Good job!," I said. "What's your name?"

He laughed. "Devan. I just hope there wasn't a camera on that corner."

"There wasn't. I checked. But that little trick won't lose them for long. Take the 405 to the 105 and then head for LAX."

Up to that point Abbie had been dutifully obeying the cell phone instruction to say nothing in front of the driver, but at the mention of LAX she could contain herself no longer. "No, Diana. I don't fly. We have tic . . ."

I put my finger to her lips. Rude, but I needed to silence her quickly. I wasn't worried about our young driver, but he might be questioned. Those few words were the first she had spoken since we met. She sounded English, probably from the London area, but I would need to hear more to be sure.

"Don't worry, Abbie. I have things in hand."

She shook her head doubtfully, but was quiet. I watched out the back window and in a few minutes I spotted them. A car speeding up the freeway toward us weaving in and out of lanes, passing all cars, searching for us. Who was the bad guy? These guys chasing us or the turkey sending us the messages. Or were they the same persons. We were only a few yards from the Sepulveda off ramp.

"Devan, exit right now on Sepulveda."

He had to cut off one driver but skillfully maneuvered us through the exit. "Great," I said. "Now go through the porte-cochere of that hotel on the right. Stay there until you see that black Buick come down the off ramp behind us. Then pull out and get back on Sepulveda and head for the airport. Abbie, as soon as we pull into the hotel duck down on the seat. Okay?"

"Okay."

I crouched down with Abbie and gave our driver one last direction. "Devan, when you get to the airport don't go to the passenger drop off, but pull into the holding area where all the limos and busses wait. Got that?"

"You bet!"

I almost laughed. Devan sounded like he was having way too much fun. "Can you see the black Buick?"

"No, not yet. Maybe we lost them when we got off at Sepulveda. Wait a minute. There they are."

"Good. Pull out. When you get to the holding lot, pull your car up behind some of the other limos as far out of sight as you can get from the entrance. The guys in the Buick may follow you in there and they may be dangerous. If they ask, tell them you dropped us off at the hotel and that's all you know. Do you understand?"

"Yes, Ma'am."

As he brought the Town Car to a stop in the lot, I handed him two bills and he thanked me, then he saw they were hundred dollar bills and he beamed. "Next time you're in town ask for me. This has been the best night I've had all month."

I said, "Abbie, climb out the door on your side and shut it quickly. Stay low and hidden by the limos. Follow me."

I climbed out my side and led us, duck-walk style, a long way up the rows of limos until I found a white Town Car, then I just opened the passenger door and Abbie and I climbed in. The startled driver was staring at us as we huddled low in the back seat, out of sight.

"Hi," I said and smiled.

He didn't smile back. He was an older fellow with grey hair and looked back at us with a stern expression. He asked, "What do you think you are doing?"

"We would like to hire your car."

"I can't do that. It's not my car, it's the company's and I'm waiting for a passenger coming in from New York."

"When does the plane get in?"

"It's not due until 9:45, but what you're asking is against company policy. I'm sorry but you'll have to get out."

Abbie was carefully peeking over the back seat and looking out the window. "They're here, Diana."

I looked out and saw the black Buick coming in the lot entrance.

"Driver, it's almost three hours before your plane gets in and we only need to go to the nearest hotel with a cab stand. You can drop us off and be back here in twenty minutes." I reached into my purse and dug out two more hundreds and tried to give them to him.

He looked longingly but said, "I'm sorry, ladies, but if I got caught, I could lose my job."

Abbie looked up at him and cried tearfully. "Please sir, that's my daughter's ex-husband in that black car. The last time he got hold of her he beat her so badly she, she lost her baby. Please," Abbie cried, "He's a mad man. I don't know what he would do if he found us in your car." Abbie took the two bills from my hand and put them in the guy's breast pocket. "Just get us out of here, drop us at a cab stand and we will all be safer."

There was a long silent pause as the driver and I sat staring at Abbie, mouths agape. I don't know which of us was more startled by her performance.

The Buick cruised slowly up the line of limos searching for us, They had never been close enough to our car to get a license or ID our young driver, and here they were confronted by dozens of identical cars. Our new driver studied Abbie a moment and then with his eyes, he began to follow the Buick as it circled closer to his car. Fear and indecision played on his face a moment then he turned forward, started the car, and said, "For God's sake stay down out of sight."

He started the car, put it in gear, and headed down the isle that would take us right past the Buick. Hiding behind the drivers shoulder, I peeked out trying to read the plate. The driver mumbled angrily, "Get down." He then continued sedately down the row and out of the lot, not even looking in the direction of the Buick.

When he dropped us at the cab stand at a nearby hotel Abbie thanked him and gave him an unwanted kiss on the cheek. He made no reply and peeled rubber getting away from us.

When we got into the cab Abbie was quick to give the driver

directions to the San Pedro harbor and the pier where our tickets said we had a ship waiting. I didn't argue. In fact, I didn't even speak. I was furious and not sure why I had a right to be. That stunt she had pulled was exactly like the stuff Jenny and I did. For us it had started as kids, listening to old *Let's Pretend* records and doing our own pretending. When we got older it turned into pranks, like sneaking into NBC by pretending to be reporter and photographer. Eventually we even used it as cover or con to get the bad guys in my PI cases. But somehow having Abbie pull it on me really ticked me off.

When we were out of the cab and walking to our pier, I asked in mock confusion, "My daughter's ex-husband who beats her? Where did that come from?"

She started to laugh. "Did you see the look on his face? It was fun, wasn't it?"

"Oh yeah, just a barrel of laughs."At that moment I realized how Jenny felt when I pulled something similar without cuing her in.

"Well, it wasn't any worse than that whopper of yours," said Abbie. "I'm a licensed PI and I have to get this woman to safety."

I had a hard time keeping a poker face when she said that. My dad was very proud of my career as a private investigator. No one could know him for more than five minutes without him whipping out the brag photos and PI stories. Yet this woman, who was supposed to he his friend, thought my PI license was a whopper.

I stared at her, a petit, gentle, lady-like woman, a damsel in distress no less. Here I was worrying about whether the bad guy was chasing me in a Buick or texting me from my Dad's cell phone, and I hadn't even considered that the main player might be this sweet, diminutive little woman I was trying to rescue. And I was about to climb aboard a ship with her.

CHAPTER THREE

As we walked down the pier toward our ship, my cell phone vibrated in my pocket. I wanted to take this message in private. "Abbie, you have the ticket info. Would you go ahead and check on it and see if those tickets are for real.? I need a moment to think."

She looked at me as if she wasn't at all sure what I was up to, but gave me a cooperative, "Sure, Diana."

I found a bench, sat down and took the call. It was not a text message or a still picture. It was a video phone call. My Dad stared back at me, alive but looking pretty beat up. He was sitting in a chair holding a New York times with today's date. Emotion whipped me in two directions, relief to see him alive and panic to see him looking so hurt and obviously still in danger.

"Dad, where are you? Are you ok?"

"I've been better, but am ok. I tried to keep you out of this, honey."

A fist appeared from off camera and punched him in the gut. "Just tell her!" said a heavily accented voice.

My nomadic childhood made me very good at accents, but I could not at that moment identify this one. I activated the capture feature of my phone so I could record the rest of our conversation.

Dad tried to catch his breath and get out the next words.

"Diana, you remember my Uncle Bennett who lived back in North Carolina?"

He knew darn well I remembered Bennett, and that I had recently been named Bennett's heir. I had been living in Bennett's North Carolina compound for the last eight months. It's true that Bennett was his uncle and my great uncle, but for him to phrase it that way meant he was trying to distance me from whatever trouble he was in. I got a queasy feeling in my stomach when I realized this would have something to do with Bennett's dangerous and clandestine life. I had spent the last eight months trying to recover some equilibrium after my first encounter with Bennett's past.

I saw a fist coming his way again. He held up one arm to fend it off and said, "I'm telling her."

The fist withdrew and he continued.

"Bennett evidently took something from these fellows and they want it back but can't find it. They did find a sort of treasure map from the late 1940's but it's all in code or riddles or something. His notes are on an old itinerary for a ship that started in Los Angeles in 1949. These guys say he got aboard with a sea chest of stuff and by the time he docked in New York, the chest was empty. They believe Bennett stashed stuff at various ports of call, but I haven't been able to solve the clues he left on the itinerary. They . . . they want you to find the stuff. That's why they planned this little junket for you and Abbie. Your ship hits the same ports of call as Bennett notes in his itinerary."

"What am I looking for? What do they want?

The guy with the thick accent said, "Turn on the iPad on the bed.".

I was confused and took a moment to answer. "What iPad on

what bed?"

Now he seemed to have a moment of confusion. Then he asked, "Where are you? Aren't you in your stateroom? There should be an iPad on the bed."

He must have not looked into the camera for fear of showing me his face. "No, I'm on the dock. I haven't boarded yet."

"Get to your stateroom. I'll call you later." He ended the call.

I pulled up the call file and forwarded it to Sam's cell. It only took two or three minutes before he called me back. "Hi, Diana. How you holding up?"

" Pretty shaken after seeing the condition Dad was in, but at least he's alive. You saw that message? And I'm still very confused. Why do you suppose they faked his death and set up this whole phony coffin thing?"

"Well, now that I've seen what they want, that's pretty clear. They couldn't find you and believe me they have really been searching. At Bennet's compound . . . no, now it's Diana's compound, security is so tight they didn't have a chance of finding you. You were totally off the grid."

"So they sent me that notice that he was dead knowing I'd surface."

"Oh, not just to your phone here. Since I got that death notice here I have been doing my own digging and I've found that notice about your Dad's death has gone out to every place you or your Dad ever lived. Phone messages left, newspaper announcements, letters, PI's hired. And of course your apartment here has been under surveillance 24/7. We haven't known if your Dad was really dead, but we were sure we had to keep a close eye on you."

I wondered briefly who he meant by *we*. Except for me, Sam

worked alone. But another thought intruded. "Oh. Now I understand why so many of the men Dad worked with were at the funeral. Wish I could have stayed around to talk with them. Sam, why do you suppose those two guys tailed me as I left the chapel? They obviously knew I was supposed to end up here at the ship."

"Either they wanted to make sure that's where you went or . . . well, there might be more than one player in this. Maybe the guys who have your Dad have competition."

"Oh, that's a happy thought. Sam, the kidnappers will hold my Dad until I find their what they want, but I'm afraid then they'll probably kill him anyway. Please do anything you can to find out where they are holding him."

"I'm already on it. I'll analyze that message you sent. Send me anymore you get. Let me know . . ."

"Sam, wait. Abbie's coming." I put the phone on speaker and slipped into my pocket.

"What's the matter, Abbie? Problem with the tickets?"

"No, no. The tickets are fine, it's just, ah, well our luggage."

"Our luggage? What's wrong with it?"

"We don't have any."

"Oh. Yes, that might be a bit suspicious. What time does the ship sail?"

"At midnight."

"Where's your suitcase? Are you at a hotel here?"

"Yes, the Renaissance in Long Beach."

"Ok, go back and tell the guy someone will be bringing our luggage before sailing time. I'll be right over."

As she walked away, I slipped the phone back out of my pocket. "You catch that, Sam?"

"I'm on it. I've got one of your special suitcases here at my place. I'll pack it and add a few special items you might need. We'll pick up Abbie's case from the Renaissance, but if you need evening wear, you better hit the ship's dress shop. If there's something else you need we'll take care of it at your first port of call. Bon voyage."

CHAPTER FOUR

The four of us stood in the stateroom, Abbie looking like she wanted to retreat in embarrassment, the porter looking tired and disinterested, the head-steward looking like he was having trouble controlling his temper, and me standing firm and determined.

The ship we were booked on, The *Roaming Dreamer*, was small by comparison with most cruise ships, and had an atmosphere of reserved elegance. It was not what I would expect kidnapers to chose to shanghai me on, but then the actions of these guys did not fit any kidnapper profile I knew. The stateroom looked quite adequate and I really had to reach to come up with a reason that our room would have to be changed.

In an adamant tone I said, "I'm sorry, Mr. Romer, but this simply won't do. My claustrophobia is a serious condition. Being in a small closed inside room would be unnerving in the extreme. I simply must have a veranda."

My real reason for refusing the room was to throw a change-up pitch at the men holding my father. They had set up this room for me, had left the iPad on the bed and probably had the place bugged. If they had anyone on board watching me, their room would be close to this one.

As Mr.Romer tried for the third time to explain that the ship was very full and no deluxe rooms with verandas were available, I had another thought. "What about a penthouse?"

He drew in a sharp breath. "Ah, that would be an upgrade of considerable cost, Ms. Hunter. Are you sure, a . . . ."

"Yes, I'm sure. Do you have one available?"

"I will have to check, but that may be possible." He stepped outside the room and made a quiet, hurried call. When he came back in he was beaming. "As it happens, the Dreamer's Penthouse with veranda is available. It's the finest room on the ship. I'm sure you will be very pleased with its amenities. Please follow me."

He ushered us into the room with a gracious wave of his arm. "This room, Ms. Hunter, is 990 square feet, which I trust is large enough that it will not bother your claustrophobia. It has a spacious living room, a dining area, a large private veranda, a guest bathroom, a large bedroom, twin beds plus a third berth, a master bath with Jacuzzi and ocean view, a separate shower, a bidet, and a walk-in closet. You have a refrigerator, a security safe, complimentary wine, spirits, soft drinks, beer and bottled water. There is also a CD player, a DVD player, a large flat screen television, cordless phone, and data port with a laptop computer for your private use. We can also set up a queen bed instead of the twins if you prefer.

I could not prevent the gloating smile. "Yes, Mr. Romer," I said. "This will do just fine."

Mr. Romer hesitated just a moment, then said apologetically, "There is only one problem. Since this room was not booked before now we do not have the personal butler service available that normally is included."

"Not to worry. Not sure I'd know what to do with a personal butler anyway. A room steward will be fine."

Mr. Romer took a deep breath and said, "Very good. Now how would you like me to bill the upgrade."

"Why, bill it to the same account that was used to make the reservation."

Romer might not have reacted but Abbie came out with a shocked, "Oh, dear."

Romer glanced from Abbie to me with a questioning look. I whipped out my platinum Amex Card and said, "I'll go with you, Mr. Romer. If you have any difficulty billing to the original account we can use mine." With the fortune Bennett had left me I could buy the entire ship and not notice the dip in my account, but I wanted to see who had booked this little excursion. If I was lucky I would come back with the account number and a way for Sam to trace whoever was holding my Dad.

I turned to Abbie who had an unreadable expression on her face. "Get comfortable, Abbie. Our bags should be here soon and we can change and go to dinner."

It took longer than expected to complete the paperwork, but by the time I was back out on the deck I had a Penthouse stateroom and a receipt with the credit account number of the guys holding Dad. No name, only letters of some company, but I hoped Sam could trace it. I went up to the forward observation deck and found a quiet spot alone to call Sam and told him what I had.

"Good job, Diana. It may just lead to a dummy account but maybe we'll get lucky. It may also piss them off. Be careful with these guys, Diana. You already know they're brutal and have a lot of resources . . . and they have your father. They might take it out on him."

I was silent for a few moments, then said, "You're right. I was focused on getting that account."

"Well, anyway. Your bags should be delivered by now and with them a little surprise. I managed to get you some backup. Watch yourself and good hunting."

I hurried back to our room wondering what sort of backup Sam could send in a suitcase. Of course, I knew the secret compartment in my bag would be loaded with the usual: extra passports, extra money, maybe one of the little plastic guns he sent me in Germany. It looked like a hair dryer until your re-assembled it, was made of space age plastic, and undetectable by metal detectors. But those things didn't normally fall under the heading of backup.

I was alarmed to see head-steward Romer in our room again. Had the owners of the account complained already? When I walked into the room he beamed me a smile and said, "Ms. Hunter, I'm delighted to tell you that due to some mix-up in orders we have a personal butler for you after all."

"Oh?" I didn't like last minute changes for unknown reasons and I didn't like the idea of having someone hanging around our room. For all I knew it could be someone working for the bad guys. "Really, Mr. Romer, that isn't necessary, in fact I don't really see —"

"Good evening, Ms. Hunter"

The voice came from the bedroom door behind me. A deep, melodic, exciting voice that I hadn't heard in over a year but would have known anywhere. I turned slowly, giving myself time to think and prepare a poker face. "Good evening," I answered.

"Ms. Hunter, I've hung some of your clothing and put some in the dresser on the left. Mrs.Winter has selected the right. However some items were a bit travel wrinkled and I thought I would take them with some of Mrs. Winter's to be cleaned and pressed. Is that acceptable?"

"Yes, that would be just fine, Mr. . . .?

"Langly, ma'am, Nelson Langly. Please just call me Nelson."

"Thank you, Nelson, and thank you, Mr. Romer, for finding us a personal butler."

Now I knew what back-up Sam had sent me and also who he meant by *we*. A little over a year ago I had been working a case and as the case grew into a full fledged financial conspiracy, I ran into Nelson working the same conspiracy from a different angle. It turned out that Nelson had served under Sam in the military. With that mutual acquaintance, Nelson and I had begun an uneasy working alliance. We made a pretty good team in more ways than one, but our jobs limited our social life to one unforgettable night in Baja.

Before my brain was engaged, my emotions sent a flush of joy throughout my body. That was not good. I was way too happy to see this guy and not just because I really needed the backup.

Our eyes met briefly, both of us having difficulty keeping recognition from showing on our faces. He looked down at the pile of laundry in his arms. "I'll take these things down to the laundry and have them back by morning. Will you be dinning in or using one of the restaurants?

"We'll try a dinning room tonight."

"Very well, I'll be back after dinner to check on you ladies and see what else I can do for you."

"Thank you, Nelson."

After Nelson and Romer left, Abbie headed for the jacuzzi tub and I looked briefly at the iPad I had carried from the first stateroom and set on the night stand. I debated taking a sneak preview before I got the call. I was emotionally and physically exhausted but mentally activated in a chaotic way. My day seemed to have been a week long. I had faced sadness and loss at my father's funeral only to be launched onto an emotional roller coaster with a new enigma at every turn. I needed to slow it all down and collect my thoughts.

I walked to the bar and poured myself a double scotch. It was Grants, my favorite. A coincidence or a gift from my "personal butler?" I could hear Abbie still splashing around in the Jacuzzi. A long heart to heart with her was on my to-do list. Could I trust her or was she here to spy on me? Was she my Dad's true lover or acting with his captors? I decided my interrogation of her could wait until after the call from the men holding Dad. I'd watch her reactions and see what could be read there before she knew of my suspicions.

The ship had started moving and I went out on my huge veranda to watch us steam through the opening in the breakwater and pass Angel's Gate lighthouse. As we left one of the busiest ports in the world, clogged with piles of containers and forests of cranes, I thought how ugly it really was. Most cities on the water, be it ocean, lake or river, look their radiant best when approached from the water. Not so with Los Angeles, largely because downtown LA is nowhere near the ocean. However, that little fact of geography didn't stop the city fathers from making Los Angeles a major shipping port. In the late 1800s several bays along the coast had been in contention for major expansion, but in 1899, San Pedro Bay Harbor was chosen and construction on the breakwater was begun. LA deftly annexed a sixteen-mile swath of land expanding LA's city limits to the harbor. LA has always been capable of taking what it wanted.

My mind wondered back to the problem at hand. What, I wondered, did Dad's captors want? Something Bennett had hidden, obviously, but that left the possibilities wide open.

My great Uncle Bennett was born in 1911, spent his youth assisting his father in a moonshine business and his teens apprenticing to his uncle Henry in New York as a watchmaker and jeweler. In addition to working in the jewelry store, he had a very lucrative side business distributing his father's high quality corn whiskey to elite clients in New York during Prohibition. When the repeal of Prohibition ended his liquor business and the deepening depression ended his career in the jewelry and watchmaking business, Bennett took a job in Germany with Deutsche Information Storage Service, DISS, a company that made punch card machines. He was only 21 and thrilled at the prospects of a good job that would allow him to travel. Unfortunately, he arrived in Germany just in time to be an eye witness to Hitler's seizure of power. He saw his German friends who supported the democracy brutally eliminated and the democracy destroyed in just three months. Rather than bolting for home, Bennett stayed in Europe and worked clandestinely against Hitler.

The end of the war should have freed him to return to a better life, but his life in the shadows never ended. There was always one more case, one more cause, one more enemy of democracy. From his hidden and highly secure home in North Carolina, Bennett continued to work clandestinely. He had a cave filled with very dangerous secrets, and for some reason I have not yet understood, Bennett chose me as his heir and successor. I received his cave of secrets, his compound and a fortune hidden in complex corporate structures. But with all of that came his enemies. Now some of those enemies had my father.

What was Bennett's secret this time? Was it plundered art stolen by the Nazis or the Russians or the Allies? I knew many such items had passed through his hands, but he held them only long enough to find the rightful owner or heir. Was it information on the relocation of the Nazi leaders who fled Germany at the end of the war? He had exposed several over the years including ones our own government had provided with sanitized Nazi records and imported to the United States. Now most were dead, but their little colonies continued in enclaves around the world. The allies may have defeated Germany and Japan, but Fascism was alive and thriving. Was it secrets of fascist influence in our own government? I had run into some of those when I first inherited his home.

My mind wouldn't let the question rest but wrestled with it eagerly. Instead of fear and dread, I tingled with excitement and curiosity. Through Angel's Gate was a new mystery, an adventure, a puzzle to solve . . . and God help me, I was running toward it with open arms. Maybe that twist in my personality was why Bennett chose me.

CHAPTER FIVE

I swallowed the last of the scotch, set the glass down on the bar, and walked into the bedroom. On the top shelf of the walk-in closet I found my little suitcase and pulled it down. I needed to check the compartment in the false bottom before Abbie emerged from her bath.

I unzipped the case and pushed the three pressure points simultaneously and opened the compartment. As expected I found false IDs and extra passports, two secure phones, and a couple ATM cards on accounts that would be secure and totally discrete from my major assets. With ATM machines all over the world I could get any currency I needed. There was also a pistol made with space-age plastic and exploding plastic bullets that were just as deadly as their metal counterparts. What surprised me, however, was that he had also provided ID and passports for Abbie. Did he trust her? Did he know something about her that I didn't. The thought that Dad might confide something so personal to Sam and not to me brought a momentary anger. Then I buried the anger and realized I needed to have a private conversation with Sam and soon.

Almost on cue my cell phone rang, but it wouldn't be Sam. Hearing Abbie climbing out of the tub, I grabbed one ATM card and one secure phone and stuffed them in my pockets. I closed the case and tossed it on the closet shelf and ran for my ringing cell phone in the living room. Grabbing the phone and the iPad, I sat on the floor where the only thing the caller would see on a video call was the yellow wall behind me.

"Hello.

I could see my Dad sitting in a chair but hear the other man's voice. "Are you in your stateroom now?"

"Yes," I answered. Then to quickly forestall other questions I added, "And I have the iPad right here. I haven't opened it yet. I was waiting for your call. What did you want me to see on it?"

Abbie, wrapped in a soft terry robe and with her hair still dripping, sat down beside me and stared at the image of Dad on the screen. Tears fell freely down her cheeks as she gazed at him. "Eddie," she whispered.

Either real sadness aged her pretty face or she was a damn good actress.

"Silence. No talking. Open the iPad and then click on the Books application."

I pushed the button to open the iPad, then slid the unlock and opened the Books. "Ok, now what?"

"Your uncle was a thief and in 1949 he stole a collection of very valuable items. None of them has been seen since. We now know that in 1949 he boarded a ship in Los Angeles and took with him a large sea chest with his stolen items. We also know that by the time he disembarked in Manhattan, the chest was empty and left aboard unclaimed. Many have searched for the valuables but until now we had no clue as to where they were hidden. Select the PDF."

This little speech was the first time the guy had talked enough for me to get a handle on his accent. I had a good ear and much travel with Dad to develop a talent for accents, but up until now the inconsistencies and lapses in this guy's speech had baffled me. Now I had him pegged. It was sheer Hollywood, a phony movie accent that identified with no specific language. His native language was undoubtedly English.

"Ok, the PDF is up. What am I looking at?"

"This document was found by us about a year ago and is the itinerary of your Uncle's voyage that he took to hide all the pieces of art. His notes are scribbled on it detailing where the items were hidden. If you want to see your father alive again, you must collect the items and return them to us."

"I don't understand. If you've had his treasure map for a year, why didn't you just get this stuff yourself. What do you need with Dad and me?"

"His notes are in code. You are his heir. Do not deny this. We have the court papers. You will know how to decode these notes and find our art."

"You've got to be kidding. If you have the probate papers you know that all I inherited was a broken down old farm house and five acres of land in North Carolina." (At least that was all that Bennett had left to be found.) "And you probably also know that the federal government seized that for back taxes and the house was mysteriously burned to the ground before I was even allowed on the property. How can I possibly know how to find this stuff?"

His answer was to viciously backhand Dad across the face. "Don't play dumb, Ms Hunter. We also know you are a very capable private investigator and very good at finding things. At least you'd better be, or your father dies. Study the first port of call and the notes. We will call back after you have left Cabo San Lucas. By then you had better have decoded your uncle's notes and found the first item."

He clicked off the phone and there was silence except for Abbie's quiet sobbing. He had said, "By then you had better have decoded your uncle's notes." Rather complicated verb tense for English as a second language. Not only was his native language English, but he was well educated. A phoney accent, an iPad, a search for a lost treasure, codes. The bastard acts like he's playing a computer game. Damn him! What sort of sick, inhumane, soulless person could treat real people like disposable pawns in a game. But damn, that's what this was like, an elaborate computer game and Cabo San Lucas was level one. My dad's life was what was at stake. Maybe this information would help Sam discover who they were.

Abbie was mumbling as she cried. "I'm so sorry. I'm so sorry, Diana."

I stiffened at the apology and looked into her red eyes and said, "It's not your fault, Abbie."

She looked at me as if she might argue that point. I saw guilt in her eyes. "Eddie wouldn't tell them a thing. He never let them know you were connected to Bennett."

As the implications of that statement hit me, the shock and suspicion made my voice louder and more angry, "You were with them?"

She jumped at my tone and cried harder. "He can't die, Diana. I have waited my whole life for a love like his. He can't die."

Heaven help me if I was wrong but I believed her. I took her in my arms and held her and quieted her crying. By the time she got the tears under control my blouse and suit were wet with tears and sticky with snot. I pulled away and got her a box of tissue from the bathroom. "Abbie, I promise you we won't let them kill him. He won't die. We can rescue my father. Are you up to helping me?"

She looked up, face red and puffy. "I will do anything!"

"Right now go wash your face and dry your hair and get dressed. We need to go to dinner."

As I went into the bathroom to clean up, I understood why Abbie took so long in the Jacuzzi. The tub looked directly out a large picture window onto the ocean. You could be stark naked and one with nature and no one could see in. Mermaid luxury. I was tempted, but had no time now. I grabbed a quick shower and got into a clean dress for evening.

Clean, made up and presentable, we headed out the door and down the hall. At the elevator I paused and said, "Abbie, I think I better go back and lock that iPad in the room safe. Would you go on down to the dining room and get us a table? I won't be long." She seemed still in a daze from the phone call but agreed. As soon as the elevator closed I pulled out the secure phone. I had kept the regular phone in its little pocket on the purse strap in case dad's kidnappers called and would hide the secure one in the back pocket of my purse. As expected Sam and Nelson were both already on the speed dial of the secure phone. Nelson picked up on first ring.

"Your wish is my command, my lady."

Did I detect a bit of resentment? Quite possibly, but no time to deal with anything but business. "Nelson, did you bring a kit to check for electronic surveillance?"

"Do you really think Sam would have let me out without it?"

"Great! Abbie and I are off to dinner. Would you please check our room and . . ."

"Yes, just been waiting for you ladies to leave."

" . . . And just for curiosity, would you also check the original room. It was . . . "

"Already done and yes, it was bugged so they may already know you moved to the Penthouse. Good news is I traced their bug and I know who they are. At least the names they are traveling under are Jake Morgan and Archie Simon. I caught photos of them and emailed to Sam. He is trying to run them down right now. Check your email. You have copies of the photos. Also good news they shouldn't even be able to get on your deck much less get a room close to you. The elevator to that deck requires a penthouse room key and both penthouse rooms are now taken. Nonetheless, I'll check your new room daily to see if they get in to set any bugs. If I find any I'll leave them in place and leave a small blue butterfly pin in the vase of flowers to give you a heads up. "

"Thanks, Nelson. I . . .it was a really good to . . . to see you and know you've got my back."

He was silent for a while and then made it clear how he felt. "Well, Diana, I owe Sam my life and when he calls, I answer."

"I . . . see. OK, well, I'll be sure to thank Sam when I talk to him." I hung up. Realizing how much left over anger he still harbored made me both sad and defensive. But I couldn't let that emotion affect our work and tried to shrug it off. I went to the room, put the iPad in the safe and headed to the dining room.

CHAPTER SIX

My suspicions of Abbie had melted away when I watched her reaction to the kidnapers' call, and over dinner, we had talked a bit of girl talk. I learned how she and Dad had met and set her straight that I really was a PI. Many more important questions would have to wait for the privacy of our room, like what happened when Dad was taken and how did Abbie end up in Long Beach, and what did she know about his kidnappers.

We were having dessert when I got an urgent and unpleasant text message from Sam. I read it and wondered if I should I tell Abbie. She was lost in thought and nibbled at her creme brulee with little enthusiasm. I didn't know her well enough to know how much she could handle. Finally, I decided she had to know for her own safety.

"Abbie, as we came into the dining room there was a large man in an ill fitting jacket waiting at the entrance. Did you notice him?"

"Of course. His jacket didn't even match his pants. Probably rented or loaned by the maitre d' to be able to get into this dining room."

Her powers of observation took me aback. "A . . . right, but there's something about him that I need to tell you. Now I don't want you to be afraid, but . . ."

In a quiet discreet voice, she completed my statement for me. "But he and that other creep who took a table just three away from us and are probably watching us for the men who have Eddie."

I stared at her open mouthed, not sure what to say next. She set down her dessert spoon and looked at me. "I may be older than you, Diana, and I may not be a private eye, but I'm not stupid and this isn't my first rodeo. What are we going to do about them?"

I laughed and shook my head. "First rodeo? From your accent I'd peg you as from a posh side of London. Didn't know they had rodeos there. You are full of surprises, Abbie."

She gave me a pert little grin. "Someday maybe I'll tell you what I was doing when I was your age. What are we going to do with those thugs?"

"Right now, nothing. I have an associate, Sam Dehany, back in San Pedro. He ran their photos through his data bases and identified them. I thought you better know they're not just surveillance, and they're very dangerous."

"Torpedoes?"

"Torpe . . . Abbie, where do you get such language?"

"Well, isn't that slang for a contract killer?"

"In the1920's maybe. But, yes, Sam thinks that's why they're here. Whether we screw up the job, or whether we finish the job; Either way, their job is probably to finish us. Right now it's okay to just know who they are and keep an eye on them.

"Now you and I need to have a long talk, but not here in the restaurant. It's too easy to be overheard. Let's go back to the stateroom. You need to tell me what happened over there, how they got Dad, what you know about them, every detail you can remember."

As we walked toward our room Abbie started to turn around. "No," I said. "Don't look. Yes, they are following us but they can't get onto our deck. Only people with special keys can get up there. Right now they're verifying that we're going to our room. Tucking us in, so to speak, so they can relax."

As we entered the room, Abbie went straight to the bedroom while I locked the safety catch on the door. I was just checking the vase of flowers for Nelson's butterfly when I heard Abbie let out a startled yell. I ran toward the bedroom as she ran out, and we collided. Behind her in the dimly lit bedroom I saw the silhouette of a tall man. I pushed Abbie aside and grabbed the nearest thing I could swing as a weapon which was a bottle of chilled wine. As the man ran out into the lighted room I set the wine back down in its ice bucket.

"It's ok, Abbie. It's just Nelson, our . . . butler."

"But he was in the bed, and . . . and snoring."

"Our bed?"

"No, Diana," said Nelson defensively."In the third berth. I was just catching a little shut eye until you two returned."

"They don't provide you fellows with your own quarters?" asked Abbie indignantly.

"I'm really sorry I frightened you, Mrs. Winters. Diana, Sam's had me on this for 36 hours straight with no sleep. I thought if I went to the crew quarters I might not wake up, and we need to talk. Have you told her . . .?"

"No. I guess it's time for introductions. Abbie, this is Nelson Langly, one of my associates. He's here to help us."

"Oh. I'm happy to meet you, or meet you properly, so to speak."

"I'm glad you're here, Nelson. Abbie was just about to tell me what she knows about Dad's kidnaping. Would you play butler and open this wine and get three glasses? Abbie, why don't you and I get into some sweats or something comfortable."

She nodded, and we both headed for the bedroom. After changing, I pulled out my secure cell phone and dialed up Sam. For the last several years Sam Dehany had been my mentor and advisor. I wanted him to hear what Abbie had to say.

Sam had spent years in government intelligence work. When the covert operations he was involved in became too immoral for him to tolerate, he migrated to a laboratory working with high-tech toys. He had spent his last four years in service developing advanced robotics technology. When he learned how his robots were to be used, however, it was the final straw. Disillusionment and disgust replaced duty and patriotism, and he decided to retire and take his robotics secrets with him. To do this, he needed to convince his superiors that he had flipped his lid and that his long awaited robots didn't work. That's where I came in. Sam needed someone unknown to his associates to help pull off his scam, and I had a reputation for using such unorthodox operations. To set up his plan, however, he also involved me with real foreign spies who didn't play nice. Needless to say, I was in over my head from the moment I said "hello" to Sam. Nonetheless, we succeeded, and Sam was able to retire. He now lives a quiet life in San Pedro and can never sell or profit from his wonderful robots. My rewards for helping him included receiving one of his robots as my personal office assistant and having Sam as my closest confident.

We all sat on the large sectional couch, and I placed the phone on the coffee table in front of us. "Abbie we will also be talking by phone to Sam Dehany, my friend that I told you about. He's going to be helping us find Dad."

"Hello, Abbie," said Sam.

"Hello," she replied. "I'm not sure what I know that can help. I wasn't there when they took him."

"Well, just tell us everything you can remember, and some of those details may help."

"Very well," she shrugged. "Eddie and I had been together in Paris and he received a cable asking him to check on an iron mine in some village in Turkey. He wanted us to go together to Istanbul on the Orient Express, not the modern one that's run by the national railways, but the luxury one created and operated by a private company. They bought all the old original cars from the 1920s and 1930s, sleeping carriages, restaurant car, and Pullman carriages, and restored them to their original luxury. When we stepped aboard that train, it was like stepping back into a time of elegance."

Impatiently, Nelson asked, "Did the kidnapers grab him on the train? How did they know you were coming that way?"

Abbie blinked, confused by the question. I shook my head at Nelson sending him a signal to let her tell it without interruption."

"Then Abbie answered, "Why no. We had a wonderful excursion from Paris, with overnight stays in grand hotels in Budapest and Bucharest and tours of both cities." She paused and looked at me. "Eddie said it should have been our honeymoon trip but this train only makes the full run from Paris all the way to Istanbul once a year, and he wanted to get back to the states and introduce me to you, Diana, before we got married."

She sipped her wine and got control of the emotions that threatened to well up. Then she shrugged again. "He put me up in the

Crowne Plaza Istanbul in the old part town and took off for his mine.
He told me he would be gone three days and gave me carte blanche to
enjoy the hotel and play tourist around the city. For three days I had a
wonderful time. The Crown Plaza has the most amazing buffet with
Turkish, European and American cuisine and the most wonderful
fresh fruit. And the people-watching was splendid. It was like being
in a movie or something with people from all over the world. It's only
a block from the tram and I saw the Blue Mosque, the Topkapi
Palace, and many beautiful . . .

Like Nelson, I couldn't stand it anymore and interrupted her.
"Abbie, please. Get to the point. What happened to Dad?"

I guess my voice had been harsher than I intended, and she
jumped slightly and looked at me sadly. Tears welled up in her eyes
and slid down her cheeks. I realized her prattle about the trip was an
attempt to hold the pain at bay.

In a tiny little girl voice she answered. "When he didn't show
up the fourth day I tried to call his cell phone but got no answer. On
the fifth day I called several times, leaving him messages each time.
No response. Finally on the sixth day I called the American Consulate
and told them Eddie was missing. I was transferred several times and
finally someone told me to come to the consulate and file a report.
Their offices were almost an hour out of town and I had to hire a car.
It took most of the day to go out there, file the report and come back
to the hotel. I didn't feel like they took the report too seriously. In
fact, I got the idea from one man there that he thought I was just
Eddie's good time girl and he'd dumped me."

At this point, Abbie broke down in sobs and we got no more
information until she could be calmed down. When she got control
and started the story again she was much more reportorial, giving us

facts without emotion or travelogue.

"I returned to the hotel about 4:30, let myself into the room and found it was torn apart, everything tossed on the floor. Astounded by the mess, I walked over to the pile and was suddenly grabbed from behind. While one man held me, another ripped my blouse sleeve and jabbed a needle in my arm. I went out very quickly and when I woke up, I was in a different room, a room that stank of filth and disuse. There was a battery powered lantern in one corner. The window was minus its glass and covered with broken boards, and you could see daylight through the openings between the boards.

I was lying on the hard floor and next to me was my suitcase. My head hurt as I rolled over, and I grabbed it and moaned. Then I heard Eddie. He said, 'Abbie, are you alright?' I sat up and saw him sitting tied to a chair. His face and body were bruised and bloody. I stood and went to him touching his cut face. I asked him who these men were and what they wanted, but he never had time to answer. They came into the room when they heard our voices.

"One of them grabbed me and pushed me into the next room. Eddie started shouting telling them leave me alone, that I didn't know anything. I heard them hit him and tell him to shut up."

Again, Abbie broke down and we waited for her to get it together. "Abbie," said Sam, "instead of thinking about all the details, try to just tell us what they wanted. Did they tell you?"

"Oh, yes, they were quite direct about that. They said Eddie's Uncle Bennett Hunter stole a treasure from their families and they wanted it back. They even had some sort of treasure map or something showing what he had hidden and where, but they had already hunted for it and couldn't find it. They believed that Eddie would be able to read the codes and clues, and they were trying to beat it out of him.

"Diana, I am so sorry. They were torturing him. I didn't think what would happen. When they said he had to know, because he was Bennett's heir, I just yelled it out so they would quit hurting him. Eddie told me to shut up but it was too late. I had already told them. Please forgive me. I didn't mean to endanger you."

"What did you yell at them, Abbie?"

When she looked up at me I saw the source of the guilt I had been reading in her. Frankly I was relieved that this is what it was about.

"I told them you were Bennett's heir, not Eddie. I'm so sorry, Diana. That changed everything. Then they wanted to know where you were. They put a knife to my throat and made Eddie tell them your address."

"What address did he give them?"

"I don't remember the number but it was in Bluff Beach."

I smiled. "Abbie, that didn't hurt a thing. The only thing in Bluff Beach is an empty loft apartment that had already been tossed by other bad guys. I haven't lived in it for eight months. And Abbie, I am very grateful to you for stopping the beating they were giving Dad."

She again dissolved into tears, but this time cried softly and they seemed to be tears of relief.

"Then what happened?"

"They gave us both knockout shots again, and the next time we woke up we were in a much nicer home, like a cabin, all by itself, somewhere in the mountains, somewhere green. Eddie said he thought we might be in Switzerland. There were just two guards and they didn't beat Eddie anymore, but every now and then they would get a telephone call and come back and ask more questions about where you and your father had lived and so forth. Eddie told them anything they asked about your old addresses. He said they were hunting for you and would never find you. Then after about two weeks, they all four came back and told me to pack my suitcase. I was going on a little trip. They knocked us out again and moved us to a small adobe house that I think was somewhere in the southwestern United States. It was dry and hot and I saw cactus and lizards and horned toads. The place was a one room dump, but for some unknown reason, it had its own private runway. Once more they knocked me out and when I woke up we were in a hotel in Long Beach. They gave me instructions about attending that funeral and told me that if you and I didn't get aboard this ship and do everything they said to do, Eddie would have a real funeral.

Before that thought could start the tears again, Sam and Nelson began asking detailed questions about the cable Dad had received in Paris, the four kidnapers and the houses Abbie and Dad were held in.

As Sam and Nelson gathered this data, I went to the bedroom and dug out the other secure phone from my suitcase and then went out on the veranda to make a private call. Nelson watched me with suspicion in his eyes, but I couldn't confide in him. I now knew enough to seek out some very secret information that might help us. Only Sam knew the secret place I was going to call, and neither Nelson nor Abbie could be read in on this one.

CHAPTER SEVEN

Our ship was anchored in the Bahia San Lucas with the blue Pacific to the west and the grey-blue Gulf of California to the north east. Abbie and I were up early and took the first lighter into town, followed, of course, by the two guys shadowing us. At least now we had names for them, even if they were aliases: Jake Morgan and Archie Simon. Jake was about 5' 10" and slender, while Archie was about 6' 6" and looked like a line backer. As our boat bounced over the swells of the bay, I could see them at the far end of our boat. It brought to mind the scene from the movie, *Cloak and Dagger*, when the killers followed the little boy on board the sight seeing boat at San Antonio's River Walk. For some reason that thought made me laugh. I have a weird mind.

Cabo San Lucas sets at the very bottom of the Baja California peninsula. As we headed for shore, our view was of bright clear skies overhead and sparkling white buildings lining the shore and climbing up the hills overlooking the harbor. The fresh smell of the sea was invigorating.

Since the 1500s it has progressed from Spanish port to pirate hangout to sleepy fishing village. In modern times it became known to the leisure class as a great sports fishing spot but they had to come by private plane or yacht because there was no land transportation and no decent accommodations. Then in the late 1940s, a bunch of Hollywood stars including Bing Crosby, John Wayne, Phil Harris and Desi Arnaz partnered up with a local man, built a hotel, and started the tourist ball rolling. In the mid 1970s, the Mexican government made roads and infrastructure improvements, and today it's one of the hottest ports of call on the Mexican coast. A tourist can find luxury hotels with infinity pools looking out to sea, spas with every sort of massage or bath you could ask for, as well as fine dining, gaiety and music.

As we walked along the streets we saw shopping ranging from street venders hanging their wares on tree limbs to high end shops that rival Rodeo Drive. There are of course many of the seamier attractions as well, including very open houses of prostitution and the availability of any drug of choice.

We had no time to enjoy Baja's tourist attractions, however, because we would have only twelve hours to search for the art Bennett supposedly left here some sixty-two years ago. I had spent last night studying Bennett's notes and the art pieces the kidnappers believed he hid on his voyage. The hints in his notes made me certain that here in Baja he had left a small Minoan statuette.

From the time we stepped ashore we were dogged by people trying to sell us everything from tourist trinkets to timeshares. As long as we kept moving it was easy to fend them off, but when we made the mistake of standing still on the sidewalk to study the map, Abbie, got the ultimate sales pitch. The *salesman* looked to be in his thirties, fairly well built and not bad looking. He sidled up behind her, caressed her bottom, ran his hand between her legs and murmured "Mama, you want some really good loving?"

Abbie stood there for a moment, her hands held in front of her chest and her face blushing bright red. Then she doubled up her right fist, whirled around and connected with the guys jaw. Her full body follow-through gave her punch much more power than I would have expected from her tiny frame and the guy landed on his butt on the sidewalk between us. As he stood up, I couldn't see his face but I could see him make a fist with both hands. He was going after her. I tapped him on the shoulder. When he turned to face me, I planted a well aimed knee that doubled him over and landed him on the sidewalk again. I knew if he got up from that one we were in trouble.

I grabbed Abbie's arm and said, "Let's get the hell out of here." We hailed a cab and climbed in. I looked out the back window to see if the guy got up to follow us. As expected, our shadows, Jake and Archie, were in the process of hailing a taxi and were going to follow. But then I saw something I had not expected. Two men approached our *salesman* and appeared to be trying to assist him, yet when he tried to pull away from them and get his own taxi they detained him, pulled him to a bench and sat him down between them. With a shock, I recognized them. They were the two men who followed Abbie and me from the funeral and chased us down the freeway. I pulled out my phone, zoomed in on their faces, and snapped off three snapshots of them. These were clear shots, though from a distance. The last shot I had taken of them from the town car had not come out. All the camera got then was a picture of their headlights.

I watched the scene behind us and Abbie gave the driver the name of a spa near the beach. He put the car in gear and headed down the street. As we pulled away I saw the two men with the salesman stand up and walk away, leaving the guy on the bench. The guy fell sideways on the bench and looked like he was out cold or maybe dead. Holy shit who were these guys? Who besides Jake and Archie were following us and why?

As we turned the corner, I lost sight of the scene but could see Jake and Archie in a taxi behind us. Before we could even get started on our search, we had to lose them. As we drove I sent the photos of the two mystery men to Sam with a short note telling him of our two encounters with them. Hopefully Sam could ID them.

Our cab dropped us off in the porte-cochere of the high-end hotel where we had reservations in their spa. Of course, Jake and Archie pulled up right behind us. It didn't matter because where we were going they could not follow. I didn't see anything more of the other two guys. We checked in and were taken to the woman's day spa which was guarded like a harem, and there we met our two massage therapists. As I handed a hundred dollar tip to each, I explained to them that I had a conflicting appointment and didn't want my boyfriend to know. I wanted to pay them to stay in the room with Abbie and not let anyone know I wasn't there. They gave me knowing smiles, certain I was sneaking off for a romantic rendevous. I didn't disabuse them of the idea. Abbie would maintain our cover here, while I met Nelson and began our search for the first piece of art.

As Abbie stripped for her massage, I peeled out of my dress and high heels revealing the bathing suit I wore underneath. I covered the suit with a white smock I borrowed from my masseuse, wrapped my hair in a brightly colored bandana and slipped on a pair of tennis shoes I had brought in my large beach bag.

"Abbie, when you finish your massage go to the women's lounge and have a nice lunch. Don't go out where our friends might see you. I'll call when Nelson and I get back and you can slip out through the pool and meet us at the car. You be okay?"

"Yes, I'll be fine. Just wish I was doing something more useful than playing decoy."

"This is not only useful, it's essential. Enjoy this quiet moment, Abbie. It may be one of the few you get on this cruise."

CHAPTER EIGHT

Nelson and I sat in his rental car arguing once again about our course of action. Abbie, Nelson and I had spent hours last night studying the notes, codes and hieroglyphics Bennett had left as clues to the location of art treasures. I had concluded that this was not really for use by someone else, like a treasure map, but was my uncle's way of making memory-joggers for himself in a sort of makeshift code in order to keep those notes private. That left a lot to guesswork and intuition. We had also examined the five photos of the art pieces the kidnapers said were hidden during Bennett's voyage and made our best guess as to which piece of art we were looking for here in Cabo.

If I hadn't spent the last eight months poring over Bennett's stash of secret files, I would have thought this whole search was some sort of elaborate snipe hunt. Actually it fit Bennett's twisted yet heroic personality perfectly. I already knew from experience that he hid information about the Nazis all over the world. I just didn't know about this art caper.

After Nelson went to the crew quarters and Abbie went to sleep, I did some computer research and was certain I had a strong lead as to were to begin our search, but that lead came from sources I couldn't tell Nelson about. The trick was how to get Nelson moving in the right direction without revealing secrets I could not expose.

Nelson pointed across the bay to El Arco, the famed arch formed by a natural rock formation just off shore. Since this was our third go-round of this argument, his voice was raised in anger. "Listen," he said, "the Hole in the Wall does refer to Butch Cassidy and Wyoming, but here on the tip of Baja, it's obvious that it has to refer to El Arco. Can't you see that?"

"Yes," I replied also with anger in my voice, "it is *obvious*, too damned obvious. Bennett was far more subtle than that and . . ."

"How can you know that? I thought you never knew this uncle of yours."

"It's so obvious that the men who have my father must have looked all over those rocks. Besides, that's one of the greatest tourist attractions here. If Bennett had hidden it out there sixty-two years ago, either some tourist would have come across it or wind and sea would have swept it away."

"Diana, why are you so stubborn about this. Is it because it's not your idea and you think you have to run the show?"

"No," I shouted in exasperation. "It's because I think it's a waste of time and we now have just eleven hours left until our cruise ship sails. You haven't even shut up long enough for me to tell you my idea."

He shouted back. "That rock may not be the hiding place but unless you at least have enough respect for my expertise to check it out, then I'll be happy to get the hell out of here and leave you on your own."

I knew he meant it. And, I knew it wasn't just this time and this argument. It was all the anger he had left over from our last case together. Either I capitulated, or he walked.

"Fine. Let's get it done quickly."

We walked up Medano Beach and tried to hire one of the many taxi boats waiting for tourists, but quickly learned that while they were willing to take us *around* El Arco, no one would get close to it because the tides were too hazardous.

After the third refusal I said, "But I've seen pictures of people walking on the sand under the arch. How do they get there?"

The boatman shrugged. "But lady, there is no sand this year. The tide is only low enough for sand during one month once every four years. You missed it. That was last year."

That little piece of information had escaped my research. I looked at Nelson. "What do you think? Is it worth our short time to take a boat around the arch?"

"No. We need a closer look at the whole rocky strip of land," he said as he started walking down beach. Five minutes later he had rented us two jet skis. Great! I had never been on one in my life and Nelson wanted to take jet skis to a place the locals said was too dangerous for a boat.

We stripped down to bathing suits and put our clothes and valuables in a locker. The vender's safety check was limited to handing us rented life vests and showing us how to start the contraption. I've noticed in countries outside the U.S., people are far less worried about things like safety belts and civil liability. You drown, it's not their problem.

Instead of making a bee-line diagonally across the harbor to El Arco, we rode along Medano Beach, past the opening to the marina and along the curved strip of land that sticks out off the end of the cape like an rocky appendix. Not only did this give me a chance to get used to my ride, but it also gave us a closeup look at the land.

The best thing that could be said for this famous strip was that it was picturesque. Other than that, it was barren and inhospitable to all but birds and sea lions. It's craggy surface has been sculpted by eons of wind and water into a bare sharp rock with pits and holes and caves. If Bennett really hid anything there, we could spend a year searching and not find it.

As our jet skis bounded, thumped, and shied through the waves and swells, I dismissed any notion that the statuette was in these rocks and mulled over what I had learned so far. I had verified Bennett's 1949 trip from Los Angeles to New York when I made my private call to Robert James Westerman last night.

Robert James had been one of my uncle's closest friends and the two of them had lived at Bennett's secret compound in the hills of North Carolina for over 35 years. Robert James served as Bennett's security manager, fellow agent, house manager, and just about anything else that was needed. In order to keep Bennett's name off the books, Robert James had also fronted as the owner of the full six hundred and forty acre section of land that was guarded by impenetrable security; while Bennett kept up the pretense of living on a rundown five-acre farm a few miles away. With the curiosity of an isolated and ingrown population, the locals had developed theories regarding who Robert James really was and where he came from and why he had this property. But he minded his own business, kept to himself and was polite and fair in all his dealing with the townspeople. After thirty years, it was only the older folk who still referred to him as "that new guy."

When I first met him I quickly learned he was a proper Englishman who would never tolerate being called just Robert or Heaven forbid, Bob, but preferred the full mouthful, Robert James.

When I inherited the compound and all the secrets and all the money, I also got Robert James in the bargain. The talented and kindly old gent was easily the best of the deal.

In my call to him last night, I told him our problem. He had searched Bennett's computer files and his diaries and had verified the trip and explained its purpose.

My problem was I couldn't let either Nelson or Abbie know about Robert James or the hidden stash of information at what was now *my* secret compound, so I had to use either real or counterfeit research to explain how I knew what I knew. *Tricky.*

As we drew close to El Arco, the water became so rough I pulled back. I thought even Nelson would see the danger but he headed right into the boiling surf. I hollered to him and signaled not to go under the arch but he ignored me, gunned the jet ski, and headed for the arch.

Waves rolled off the Pacific and crashed around the rocks near the arch and were met by a defending surge from the gulf. I yelled at the top of my voice, "Nelson, at least hang back and time the waves." He didn't hear me. He was playing tourist looking at the walls and roof of the arch when a giant wave burst through. I saw his jet ski rear up, then he and the ski were covered by the wave. When the wave receded, both he and the ski had disappeared.

I let out an involuntary scream, "Nelson!" I gunned my jet ski and headed for the narrow channel between the eastern pillar of the arch and the next big chunk of rock, but as I got closer I saw the waves and turbulence were as great there as under the arch. I turned toward the tail of the formation and found less turbulent water on the far end. Pushing the speed on the jet ski, I raced around the rock. I could feel the involuntary suppression of my emotions, a quiet and calm that comes over me in any real emergency. I don't understand it, but I know it helps me function.

Searching for Nelson and his ski and fearing what I would find, I surveyed the water and the rocks. At first I saw nothing, then with gut wrenching certainty I identified bits and pieces of the jet ski being pounded against the jagged rocks. Among them I saw Nelson's bright orange life vest.

"Oh, God no, please. Nelson!"

I tried to push my jet ski closer for a better look but waves from the Pacific buffeted me and I had to turn into them to keep from being rolled onto the rock myself. As I turned into the wave and looked out to sea I caught a small motion, a white arm raised above the green sea. With joyous relief, I realized Nelson was out past the breakers. He must have dived under the waves and swam out. I timed the next wave and headed toward him during the calm.

He climbed up behind me, almost tipping both of us off and sat breathing hard and looking exhausted.

"You alright?"

He saved his breath and just nodded.

"How did you lose the life vest?"

"Had to jettison it to dive under the waves."

"Hang on," I said and headed out around the rocks to calmer water and across the bay to Medano Beach.

As the fear and adrenalin subsided, anger at his pig-headed stupidity took over. By the time I docked the ski, I was furious. To keep from pounding on him, I turned away. "You lost that other jet ski. You can leave it on my credit card, but you explain to the vender what happened and how incredibly stupid you were."

With that I huffed off. While he took care of paying for the ski, I returned my vest, opened our rented locker and retrieved our clothes and my large beach bag. As we sloshed up the beach in wet tennies, Nelson avoided discussing his stupid ride under the arch by belaboring his assumption that the rocks were the hiding place.

"We still need to look in those rocks more carefully. Maybe we could go to Lover's Beach and climb over the rocks to the arch . . ."

"No, we can't. We're now down to 10 hours until our cruise ship sails."

He wouldn't give it up. "Maybe we could hire an ultra-light aircraft and fly over the rocks . . . but they are full of caves. Your uncle could have hidden the statute in any of them. It's impossible."

"Ya think?"

"Damn it Diana, you have been real good on the negativity side, where do you think he hid it? And by the way, why are you so sure it's the Minoan bull dancer statuette instead of one of the paintings. Those guys gave us pictures of five pieces of art and we have six ports of call before we hit Manhattan. Why do you think the bull is here.?"

"Oh, good questions! Does that mean you're ready to listen now, or will I just be insisting on my way again?"

He stopped, put his hands on his hips, and looked at me with an indescribable and unreadable expression. Then he looked around the street and pointed to a coffee shop with sidewalk seating. "Let's sit and have a hot coffee and a pastry and you tell me about it."

Our chairs were side by side and our shoulders touched. Even after his dunking in the ocean, I could smell his lingering aftershave. Nelson's closeness and the taste of the strong rich Mexican coffee conjured up sudden memories of our last trip to Baja together.

Vividly I remembered lying in the bed in the cabana, feeling the soft sea breeze blow in through the open louvers across our entwined bodies. The unexpected memories overwhelmed my emotional defenses. *Not good, not good.* I couldn't go there now. I had to concentrate.

I placed my large beach bag and the table between us and used the motion as an excuse to move my chair slightly away from his. Pulling out the iPad, I opened it to the page with Cabo San Lucas and set it on the table facing Nelson. I pointed to Bennett's notes on the top of this page: "Hoped for good weather, **but** **l**ooks **l**ike rain."

Nelson nodded.

"Look at the letters carefully. Some of them are darker as if the pen leaked or he wrote over the letters twice."

"Well, the b in 'but looks darker,' I guess."

"Look again. What other letters are dark?"

"The u in 'but' and the two ls in 'looks' and 'like.' Okay, those letters spell bull but are you trying to tell me that's his code? That's nothing but a coincidence, an accident in writing."

"Yes, that's what most people assume when they see such writing inconsistencies, especially with old fashioned, leaky pens, but Bennett didn't make accidents. Everything he wrote had a purpose."

Nelson looked at me, his green eyes showing doubt. Then as he studied my face, suspicion grew in his. "I thought this was the great uncle you never knew."

I smiled and looked down at my hands. "I met him only twice when Dad took me to visit his little farm. However, he was the only family we had. Dad and I both carried on a correspondence with him over the years, and I came to know many of his codes."

"Many of his codes? What was this guy, a spy or something?"

"He was a farmer, a farmer who raised corn and made illegal sour mash whiskey. He, and his father before him, made very good quality booze, not just raw white lightning, but aged sour mash whiskey. But even after Prohibition ended it was still illegal for him to make his own whiskey, and I guess he got in the habit of using codes for his own protection. Maybe it was just a game, but that's how he wrote. Now can we get back to the problem at hand?"

He stared at me a long time. "Nothing changes. You're scratching your head at the back hair line. That's one of your tells. You're lying to me, Diana. Again. Just like last year. I guess I should expect it of you. I'm not stupid. I looked up this art work we're tracking and I know for sure at least one piece is Nazi loot from World War II. How did a corn farmer from North Carolina get hold of it? And how did he end up hiding it all over the globe when he was on a cruise?"

I stared back at him, trying to decide what he had a right to know and what I dared tell him. I could tell him nothing about the compound and nothing about Bennett's clandestine career of Nazi hunting. If I limited the tale to this treasure, it might be enough to gain his trust. Even that much, however, would require some creative facts.

"I'll tell you all I know about this treasure, but since my information comes from old letters he wrote to my dad, it really isn't much. Bennett had been working in Europe after the end of the war, and he learned that a U.S. Army officer in charge of guarding a large hoard of Nazi treasure had helped himself to some of the better pieces. Bennett wasn't able to prove it, and there was nothing he could do at the time, but it galled him. He decided he would track the art, steal it back, and return it to its rightful owners or their heirs. He was able to track the art to the officer's home in Texas. Then Bennett and his friend, Otto Brehm, stole it back but they couldn't find records of the owners.

"Of course, back then, he didn't have computers and internet and all the lost art web sites that we do now. I think if we can recover this stuff, we might be able to complete his quest. But first we have to rescue my Dad, and I really need your help. You with me?"

"Why didn't Bennett just turn the guy in?"

"You remember that case you and I worked together? The criminals we were after were too powerful and too well connected. We couldn't get them by normal legal prosecution. That's the situation Bennett was in. The officer who stole the art was high up the ranks of the OSS and was also an important player in Washington D.C. Bennett never told Dad who it was. He just said that if he filed a complaint, he would have been the guy to go to jail."

"Why didn't he hide the stuff in one place? Why take a cruise?"

"He and Otto were being chased after they stole the art, and they didn't take a cruise. They hopped the *J. H. Harden*, the first freighter leaving port in Los Angeles and worked their way back to New York. They wanted the art hidden before they got back and not in one place where it could easily be found."

"So, why didn't he come back for the treasure in all those years."

"I don't know. Maybe he never found the owners, maybe he forgot."

Suspicion gleamed in his green eyes again. He didn't raise the volume of his voice, in fact, he spoke in just above a whisper, but the intensity of his emotion went up many decibels. "And you just happen to remember all this from letters written to your dad decades ago, before you were born? Diana, why do you have to do this? I'm your partner in this case, not the bad guy. Why can't you be honest for once? Why do you have to hold your cards so close to your vest? What else do you know that you haven't told me that could help us find this bull?"

"I don't *know* anything, but I do have a guess or two." He shook his head rejecting my words before I could finish my answer.

I held up the iPad and started flashing pages of researched documents past his face. "And not just from memory of old letters. I started with what I remembered, then did research last night after you went to bed. Look here. Bennett's notes are from the *J. H. Harden*. This is the ship's record from the Maritime Museum in Los Angeles. Notice that Bennett's freighter made the same ports our cruise does."

Finally his eyes focused on the page. He flipped back and forth between Bennett's itinerary and the ship's record. When he was satisfied they matched he gave me sheepish look and said, "I'm sorry, Diana."

I had, of course, gotten the information from Robert James and backed it up with material from the Maritime History Library, so I couldn't really gloat too much over his apology. "I tried to tell you some of this before our wild ride to El Arco. Finish your coffee and we'll get the car and I'll tell you my guess as to where the bull is hidden on the way to our next stop."

CHAPTER NINE

After her massage, Abbie went to the women's lounge as instructed. There were no single tables and she had been seated with three other woman. She sat quietly, trying to visit as little as possible, partly because she was preoccupied with thoughts of Diana and Eddie, and partly because she was not thrilled with her table company.

Abbie's companions included Shirley and Katherine, two older heavy-set ladies whose husbands were fishing together, and Judy, a gorgeous well built brunette with a heavy Bronx accent. Katherine had jewels around her neck, on her ear lobes, and on almost every finger, and she displayed her monied-class arrogance just as conspicuously as the jewels. Currently she was grumbling about the lunch, a seafood salad with fresh tropical fruit. The presentation was grand, but the portions small.

She called the waitress over, addressing her as "You there, girl," and preceded to yell at her. "The portions of this salad were hardly fit for an appetizer, and you're charging me eighteen dollars for a couple of shrimp and a few bites of melon? You really see the tourists coming don't you. Well don't think because I'm am American and I wear diamonds you can get away with this. You think . . ."

Nervously the girl tried to apologize and placate the woman. "I'm very sorry, Ma'am. What else would you like? I can get you another salad or something else, at no charge, of course."

"And wait forever for you to bring it? You certainly took your sweet time getting the first one out to me. How long did it sit in the kitchen before you picked it up?"

"I am so sorry. I can put a rush on anything you would like."

Katherine took another breath ready to continue her tirade, but Abbie could stand it no longer. Addressing the girl by name and handing her a twenty dollar tip, Abbie said, "Louisa, my dear, my lunch was delicious and your service delightful."

The girl thanked her, took the twenty and made a hasty retreat. Katherine glared at Abbie, trying to take her measure, but she said nothing. Abbie appeared secure enough to fight back.

Shirley embarrassed by the scene, tried to fill the gap with conversation. "I remember the last time we were here, Katherine. We stayed in a small cabin and . . . "

Katherine pounced. "We did not. What's the matter with you, Shirley? Get your head on." Shirley blushed and looked down at her tea glass. She was not as ill mannered as Katherine, but she had her own problem, one she could barely cope with. Her memory was failing in early senility. Unfortunately, she was not so far gone that she could not be embarrassed when she made a memory error. When Katherine corrected her, Shirley was silent a moment, then started another story. She had reached the stage of senility where she would tell familiar stories, ones she still remembered well, and would repeat them in an endless loop. For the third time that lunch, she started on a story of her and her husband's first fishing trip to Cabo. "When Charles and I first came to Cabo we had to come by private yacht because there were no roads and no planes, and we stayed at a famous hotel owned by Bing Crosby . . . "

Katherine slammed her hand down on the table. "For Christ's sake, Shirley, will you shut up? That's the third time this morning you've told that same story."

Shirley jumped when Katherine slammed the table, then looked like she might cry.

Abbie stood and picked up her small fanny pack. "Shirley, I'm going to the hot tub for a while. Would you like to join me?"

Shirley looked at Abbie, confusion and perhaps fear showing on her face. Then she looked at Katherine as if seeking permission but Katherine shook her head in a silent but firm negative. Shirley looked back to Abbie and said meekly. "No thank you."

Judy jumped up and said, "I'll join you." As Judy picked up her purse she leaned over the table and spoke directly to Katherine in a low voice. "Ya know, bitch, I'd rather listen to your friend's stories all morning than hear the rude nasty shit that comes out of your mouth."

Katherine looked shocked, but offered no response other than a hateful glare. As they walked away, Abbie started to giggle. Judy looked at her defensively.

"Good for you, girl," said Abbie. "I would like to have given that old bag a piece of my mind, too."

"Well you did good by that waitress. I liked that. I used to be a waitress. I know what it's like."

"You were? What do you do now?"

Judy pointed out the window to the pool. "See that big man in the chair under the pool cabana?"

Abbie looked out and saw five men all in business clothes

sitting in the shade of a private pool-side cabana. "Which one? Why aren't they in bathing suits?"

Before Judy could answer, Abbie heard a disturbance from the other end of the woman's lounge in the direction of the massage rooms. There were men's voices raised in anger.

"The one facing this way," answered Judy. "Like he's the king and the rest of those guys are waitin' on him." She laughed. "Which is sort of like it is."

Abbie, now dividing her attention between Judy and the ruckus at the door, asked, "And what do you do for him?"

Judy gave her a smile. "Anything he wants. He takes good care of me."

"That's nice," answered Abbie absently. "And what does he do?"

Judy laughed. "He's in pharmaceuticals."

Something in her tone of voice made Abbie withdraw her attention from the commotion at the door and focus on Judy. The pretty woman's face held a wry smile as if she'd made a joke and was waiting to see if Abbie would get it. Abbie looked out to the collection of very rough looking men in the cabana and the meaning of "pharmaceuticals" registered. "Oh, drugs. That seems to be a big business here."

The voices at the door were now louder and there were two women yelling back. One heavy deep male voice said, "No massage takes two hours. Either you let me in, or I'll bust in this door."

By then everyone in the lounge was looking toward the door and muttering. Abbie pulled Judy toward the side exit that led to the pool. "Judy, I think those two men pounding on the door may want to speak with my friend . . . and with me. My friend is a woman about your height, build, and coloring. If they were to chase you, would your boyfriend and his friends at the pool protect you?"

"You can bet your galoshes they'd protect me. Why?"

"I'm going to go out this door and out of the pool enclosure and try to get away from the men at the door. If you wait here at the pool door, but not show them your face, they might think you're my friend and . . ."

"I gotcha, Mama. Get going. My guys'll take care of things."

With nothing but her bathing suit, coverup, sandals and fanny pack, Abbie slipped though the door, across the end of the pool enclosure and out of the pool gate. Then she looked around for a taxi or bus or any form of transportation. She saw only sand. She knew there were taxi boats down by the water, and she was sure there would be taxis in front of the spa, but she wasn't sure how much time she had before the two thugs discovered their mistake and came after her.

Then, with a gust of wind and sand, the answer to her problem presented itself. A small ultra-light plane landed just a few yards down the beach from her. It looked like a dragonfly and sounded like a lawn mower, but it seemed to fly. Racing for the craft before anyone else hired it or it took off again, she simply climbed aboard without asking any questions. The pilot looked at her with some surprise and asked, "Where would you like to go?"

Abbie took a quick look back at the pool gate. The two thugs from the cruise ship came out the gate, but not of their own volition. They were tossed out and landed on their faces in the sand. Four of Judy's friends followed them, pulled them to their feet and beat on them.

Abbie smiled and answered the pilot. "Up," she said.

"Anywhere away from here."

CHAPTER TEN

Nelson and I were parked in front of the magnificent entrance to La Vida Cabo, a palatial resort hotel. Water tumbled musically down seven levels of native rock into a reflecting pool at the bottom. The entire fountain was surrounded by an oasis of palm trees. Steps circled around both sides of the fountain oasis leading to gold plated doors that sparkled in the sun. Nelson looked at this place I had insisted we go and shook his head.

"Diana, this place wasn't even built when your Uncle came through here. How on earth could you believe he hid that statue here?"

"I don't know how or where, but I am sure his hiding place has something to do with this property. Look, you have to see this place as he saw it in 1949. Figure what was here then, and go from there.

"After World War II, the Hollywood crowd discovered that this area offered both great fishing and seclusion because there was no road this far down the peninsula and no air service. You had to have a yacht or a private plane to get here. By 1948 a local fellow named Abelardo L. Rodrigues Montijo realized his large acreage and five miles of private beach just south of La Paz would make a great resort. He and his wife started building small cottages and before long they had a bunch of Hollywood partners. Bing Crosby, Desi Arnez, John Wayne, Phil Harris and others built a large hotel known as Las Cruces Hotel because it stood where Cortez had placed three crosses.

"By the time Bennett got here in 1949 the tourist building boom had begun. The ship he was on was bringing lumber and other building supplies and Bennett evidently got acquainted with a guy named Ramon Montoya who was developing a piece of land between Cabo San Lucas and San Jose del Cabo and . . ."

"And how, pray tell, did he get to know this guy and hide his little treasure in a one-day layover in this place?"

"Think, oh impatient one. He wasn't on a cruise. He was on a freighter that took two days to unload its shipment for this port and three days to find another shipment to carry to ports south."

Nelson opened his mouth but before he could ask how I knew that I said: "The Marine History Museum Library."

Instead he asked, "Diana, what makes you think Bennett knew this guy or had any connection to a hotel that wasn't built until 1968?"

"If you'd quit interrupting, I could tell you. I don't know how he met Ramon but at that time Ramon was just building little cottages. The hotel was far in the future." I opened the iPad and was pulling up the corporate records to show Nelson when my phone rang. I had given Abbie one of my secure phones and I had the other one.

"Hi, Abbie. What's up?"

"Well, our friends from the cruise ship got tired of waiting and broke into the women's lounge and . . .

"Abbie, are you alright? What is that motor noise I hear?"

"Oh, I'm fine. Those men aren't so great, but that's a long

story. Tell you later. The motor is an ultra-light aircraft, and I need to know where you are so I can have this guy fly me there before we run out of gas. Where are you, and did you find anything yet?"

"No, not yet. Ask your pilot if he knows where the La Vida Cabo resort is."

As the pilot yelled over the noise of the motor I could hear his answer. "Oh, yes. I know where it is but it is a very exclusive private resort, members only." Then after a pause, he added, "with a very strict dress code."

My guess was Abbie didn't look dressed for it. "That's okay, Abbie. Have him drop you here in front. You'll see us and the car."

When I hung up and turned back to Nelson, he had been looking at the pages of the iPad that I had turned to and was giving me that angry green-eyed glare again.

"Oh good," I said, trying to ignore the anger I saw on his face. "You saw the pages of research and Bennett's name as one of the original investors in La Vida Cabo."

"Yeah, I saw it. I suppose this is more research you just happened upon at the Marine History Library."

"Happened upon? Research I happened upon? Is that really how you think I do my work? Have you forgotten that it was my ability in documents research that helped us nail those crooks in the last case we worked together?"

"And when the hell were you going to tell me about this, Diana? After I damn near drown out there at El Arco?"

"Don't you dare try to put that one on me. I tried for twenty minutes to tell you, and you wouldn't hear of it. You said if I didn't go out to El Arco you were quitting me. You wouldn't even listen. You just kept insisting that it had to be out at El Arco so you could get your damn thrill ride. And I might point out, it was me who had to save your ass."

"Okay, Wonder Woman, if you weren't hiding this all the time, tell me how and when you found this little bit of information."

"Last night I used the laptop in my suite to tie into my office databases and search every place I could think of that might tie Bennett to Baja. I found this in California State Corporations records. No big mystery."

Of course the absolute truth of the search was that I assigned it to Yeabot, my robot that Sam had made for me because Yeabot can search, screen and filter millions of bits of data in a fraction of the time it would take me. There, again, was one more secret I had to keep from Nelson, not because I didn't trust him, not because I didn't value him as a partner, but because of loyalty to another partner, Sam.

Now cold and distant, Nelson said, "For arguments sake let's say I somehow prevented you from telling me about this. Well, now I'm listening. Is there anything else, anything whatsoever that you either know from past history with your uncle or have learned through your brilliant research ability that I should know about finding this statue? How does knowing your uncle was once a partner in this place in 1949 help us find a statue more than sixty years later?"

Before I could answer an ultra-light landed, blowing dust up around us. Abbie alighted from the little craft, paid and tipped her pilot and ran across the parking lot to us. Then the three of us huddled in the car to plan our assault on the glittering resort.

I brought Abbie up to date and answered Nelson's question. "I don't know whether it will help us or not, but I know he bought into this place with a partner named Walter Hengst and has remained on the corporate records right up until last year when he died. Some of these records refer to specific square footage, as if he bought one of the early cottages. If we can find out what he invested in, maybe we can figure out where to search. The trick is going to be finding someone with enough knowledge to help us dig out this information."

We climbed the stairs, entered through the golden doors and stared in awe. The atrium lobby rose seven stories. The circular walkways at each level dripped with green vines and brightly colored tropical flowers. In the center of the lobby stood a marble goddess holding an urn and pouring out water that flowed beneath the floor, through a glass covered channel, out the door and down to feed the waterfall at the entrance. The scents of perfumed flowers and damp earth enhanced by the sounds of running water created the ambiance of a tropical paradise.

Everyone in the place was dressed for elegance, and there we stood like unsightly flotsam and jetsam washed in on high tide. Abbie and I were both in bathing suits covered with shear cover-ups, and Nelson was in shorts and a rather ragged t-shirt. All of us had dirty, sandy shoes. Most of those around us took a quick shocked look, then avoided making eye contact. A desk clerk stared directly at us and picked up the phone. In moments a tall strongly built fellow came out of the back office, motioned to two security types and headed our way.

"Don't think we're going to get anywhere dressed like this." I took both Nelson and Abbie by the arms, ushered them into a quick about-face, and marched us back out the front entrance.

As we walked across the parking lot to our car, I searched the iPad. "Nelson, there is a shopping center at San Jose del Cabo called The Shoppes at Palmilla. Supposed to be very chic. More importantly, there is an office supply and copy center there. Let's class up our act and then hit this place again."

CHAPTER ELEVEN

Attorney Nelson Langly approached the desk. He was dressed in a three thousand dollar suit and was carrying an expensive attache case filled with printouts of all the corporate documents I had found. Handing the clerk his freshly minted business card, he said, "Miss Hunter and her Aunt Abbie are here for their 1:30 appointment with Mr. Renaldo." This, of course brought a blank look to the clerk's face, then a quick smile.

"Of course, sir. One moment please."

As the young clerk turned to his supervisor, Abbie and I, elegantly dressed, seated ourselves on a nearby divan to watch the show. The senior clerk of course had no better idea than the younger one as to what this was about. But since we had done our homework and had invoked the name of the head honcho of this place, the senior clerk quickly approached Nelson with a gracious smile.

"Good afternoon, Mr. . . ." he looked down at Nelson's card. "Mr. Langly. I am Mark Sanchez. I understand you have a meeting with Mr. Renaldo? I'm sorry, but I don't seem to have any memo on this. Could you tell me, please, what this is concerning?"

"Certainly," said Nelson agreeably. "My client, Ms.Diana Hunter is the heir to her uncle's estate. A couple months ago we called and made an appointment to speak to Mr. Renaldo about

Bennet's holdings here at La Vida Cabo because our records on this holding are somewhat incomplete."

Sanchez's face went blank. "I'm sorry sir, but I do not know anything about an owner named Bennett."

Nelson's tone altered from agreeable to slightly impatient and a bit superior. "Of course you don't, Mr. Sanchez. This is a matter we need to take up with Mr. Renaldo. That is why we made the appointment with him. Now our cruise has only a short layover here. Could you please simply take him my card and let him know we are waiting for our appointment, and we have a limited amount of time in this port."

Sanchez maintained a slightly cold stare for only a moment, then with a tight little smile replied, "I will tell him."

Sanchez was gone for a long while and I began to fear our little ruse wasn't going to work. Then a large portly man came out to the front desk with Mr. Sanchez. He greeted Nelson warmly, shook his hand, and then in a booming voice said, "I am so sorry, Mr. Langly, but I have no record of this meeting and no knowledge of an owner named Mr. Bennet. I'm not sure how I can help you."

Of course this was Nelson's cue to pull out his corporate records and worm his way into Renaldo's office for a private chat. As he handed the documents to Renaldo he explained, "It's not Mr. Bennett. The name is Bennett Hunter and he has been an owner here since the first cottages were being built."

Light dawned on Renaldo's face and he began looking through the documents. He boomed out, "I'll be damned. The mysterious Mr. Bennett Hunter. He really existed? He's been on that corporate printout longer than anyone can remember, but no one has ever seen or spoken to him."

After leafing through the documents, Mr. Renaldo handed them back to Nelson. "I'm sorry, Mr. Langly, but my job here is to manage the resort. I really have no knowledge of corporate. Not even the current corporate business falls under my purview, much less this. This is ancient history. You will have to see someone at corporate, and I'm not even sure whether you should talk to the office in Los Angeles or Mexico City."

Nelson began pointing out the square feet description in the documents, hoping it would jar loose some information but I lost track of their conversation because my attention had been taken by a tall, slender, woman crossing the lobby behind Nelson. She had been walking with grace and elegance across the lobby toward the dining room but stopped abruptly and whipped around to look toward the registration desk when she heard Renaldo boom out the name Bennett Hunter. She was thin and probably in her mid-fifties. Her skin was pale and unwrinkled but her black hair had started to grey at the temples and forehead. If cast in a movie she would certainly have been addressed as Dona. She turned and listened as Nelson and Mr. Renaldo continued their conversation. Her emotions showed clearly on her face, and it was obvious she was distressed by what she heard. As Renaldo was giving Nelson a firm and final brush-off, she seemed to make a decision. Though her facial expression registered anguish and reluctance, she approached Nelson as he turned away from the desk.

She placed a tentative hand on his sleeve and asked, "Senor, you are the heir of Bennett Hunter, yes?"

Surprised by her, Nelson said, "What?, er no. Ah, Diana Hunter is his heir. Do you know something about him?"

She smiled a sad smile. "A little," she said. "Could I perhaps meet this Diana Hunter?"

I stood and walked over to her, my hand extended. "I'm Diana Hunter, and you are?"

As she shook my hand she said, "I am Grace Irene Hengst Williamson. *Con mucho gusto*, Miss Hunter."

"It's my pleasure, Senora Williamson. This is my aunt, Abbie Winter, and my attorney, Nelson Langly. She shook their hands and we all stood silent a moment. Then I asked, "Is there perhaps somewhere we could talk?"

She hesitated a moment, then asked shyly, "Do you all like seafood?" When we said yes, she addressed the restaurant maitre d' by name and gave him instructions in Spanish to have Cabo seafood enchiladas prepared for four and served as soon as possible in her home. Then with a slightly imperialist snap of her fingers she summoned a young bellman and instructed him to bring a golfcart to the side door to convey the four of us to her home.

CHAPTER TWELVE

The heavy wooden beams in the central part of the house were intricately carved and reminded me of the Bavarian chalet my uncle had built in Germany, but the rooms surrounding it were all Spanish hacienda style with adobe walls that were two feet thick. I studied the incongruity while Grace poured us all wine.

As she handed me a glass it became obvious that I too wore my thoughts on my face for she said, "Yes, this house has a German heart but is dressed as a Mexican lady."

She spoke excellent English with no real accent. The only thing that gave away that she had learned it as a second language was that it was too perfect, lacking slang and contractions.

"That is because when my father first started to build this house in 1949, he still missed his homeland. But over the years, this became his home. And he also built the additions more for my mother's tastes."

She had seated us in a lovely large livingroom with a wide picture window looking out to sea. Her house was the largest one we'd seen on our ride up the hill from the hotel, and it sat directly on the pinnacle of the whole property. The view of the town and the sea was magnificent.

"So, your father was from Germany, but settled here. What

caused him to emigrate so far from home?"

"That is a long and boring story. To make it short, something happened in Germany that forced him to leave."

"What was that?"

She studied me a moment as if she was debating the answer. "Does the date, November 9, 1938, mean anything to you?"

I thought a moment, going mentally through my uncle's diaries from his years in Germany and then it hit me. "*Kristallnacht.* The night of Broken Glass. The Nazi attack on synagogues and other Jewish places. Was your father a Jew?"

"No. He was just a good German boy who believed in justice and made the mistake of fighting for it. He thought the attack in his home town of Bremen was just some local thugs and hooligans. He and his cousin, Alfred, tried to protect some Jewish friends and ended up beating some Nazis quite badly. By the time they found out the attack was official policy, the Nazis were scouring the town looking for them. Father and Alfred hid out that night in the bell tower of the Lutheran church and laughed as they watched the Nazis running all over town looking for them. They stayed there the next day too, getting quite hungry. Then their situation became more dire. They learned one of the Nazis they had beaten had died and they were wanted dead or alive. There was only one thing for them to do. That night they slunk down to the docks and signed on as crewmen on a Spanish ship that sailed with the evening tide. Both being carpenters, they got good assignments as apprentices to the ship's carpenter."

"That's not a boring story at all. What a sudden change in his life. How did he end up living here?"

"Well, by 1943 he had been at sea for five years. The war was raging, he had no chance what-so-ever of going home and the merchant marine business had become quite deadly due to Nazi submarines. But I guess what really did it was, he was ashore here and met my mother. They fell in love and somehow he never left this place."

"That's a wonderful story, and one my uncle would have appreciated. I noted that one of your names was Hengst. In some of my uncle's papers he referred to a Walter Hengst here in Cabo. Was Walter your father?"

She stiffened just a bit and gave me a tight smile. "Yes."

"So I am right that they knew each other. Do you know how they became friends?"

She smiled again, this time with some real humor. "As I heard the story, it was language that brought them together and a bottle of whiskey that made them friends. My father was the head carpenter for Ramon Montoya who was building this development, just putting up the first cottages back then. When your uncle's ship came in my father did not get the materials he wanted and went to talk with the captain. The captain was American and spoke only a few words of Spanish and no German. Your father overheard the communication difficulties and helped settle the problem. Then the story goes, my father took your uncle on a tour of Cabo, and that night they took a large bottle of very good whiskey to the beach, and by morning the whiskey was gone and they were fast friends."

We all laughed and I asked, "And business partners?"

Grace quit laughing and looked at me angrily. "Are you toying with me, Miss Hunter?"

Alarmed by the anger in her tone I tried to reassure her. "No. Not at all. What have I said?"

Before she could answer there was a knock at the door. Her

maid answered, and soon the waiter and maid had a delicious smelling lunch laid out on the dining room table. We all sat, but Grace's feelings of anger and distress so permeated the room that none of us did much eating. Grace didn't even lift her fork but did begin to answer my question.

"Yes, my father and your uncle struck a deal. By then my father had his Mexican citizenship and could buy land and he had the skills to build, but he had no money. Your uncle had money. Together, they built this house."

"So this house was Bennett's only investment here?"

"I'm so sorry if it is such a great disappointment to you," she snapped.

"No, that's not it at all. It's a wonderful home." I was frantic that everything I said seemed to make her angrier and I didn't understand why. "It's just that we, we're looking for something and thought that . . ."

She looked up at me as if she had been in a different world, then looked back down at her plate and began to mumble. "We always knew the day would come, of course. It's right there in their contract. My father was the one who insisted the clause be in the contract." She let out a sad laugh. "And you would never have known if I had kept quiet. But then I wouldn't be my father's daughter. I had to speak up."

She looked back and asked, "How much time do I have? When will you need it?"

Still confused, I asked, "You know what we have come for?"

"Of course I know what you've come for. I am not stupid."

"Well, if it's not too much trouble, we really need it before the ship sails at 7 P.M."

She slammed the table with an open palm. "By 7 today? Are you crazy? It will take me months to even figure out what to do with our family belongings. Two generations have lived in this house. My father's no longer alive. He can't build the second house now. I don't care what they wrote in that contract. You can not just take our home like that."

"Take your home? What on Earth are you talking about? I don't want to take your home."

She looked into my face for a long time and then asked, "Then what are you here for? What are you talking about?"

I was so relieved to realize that there was a misunderstanding that I almost laughed, but as upset as Grace was that would not have been good.

"Grace, why do you think we are here to take your home?

"Because that is what they agreed. My father would use the money your uncle gave him to build two houses. He could live in the first and build the second one later when Bennett came back to Mexico. But Bennett never returned. He just kept telling my father to use the cash for additions on this house. When I heard talk of Bennett Hunter's estate I thought . . ."

"And your family has lived under that threat all these years. I am so sorry. I am sorry we caused you such distress. Believe me, what I want has nothing to do with your home. When Bennett was through here in 1949 he had something that was very valuable, and he was looking for a place to hide it and keep it safe. I thought if I found out what he invested in, I might also find the statuette he left somewhere here. It was a piece of Minoan art, a small statue of a woman holding onto the horns of a bull and leaping over . . .

"You want Jo Jo?"

"Jo Jo?"

"The bull dancer, that is what we call her, Jo Jo."

"Yes, do you know where it is?"

Grace pulled her napkin from her lap, put it to her face and began to cry great sobs of relief. In between sobs she said, "Yes, I know where Jo Jo is."

Nelson, who had been absolutely quiet though this terrible conversation, now said, "Yeah, Diana, I think I know where it is too. You see that painting on the wall, two red rock formations rising out of the Wyoming grassland. I'd bet my last dollar that is the Hole in the Wall hideout and that there is a safe behind that picture. Is that right, Grace?"

In a not so lady-like way, she blew her nose loudly on the napkin and answered, "You are partly right, Mr. Langly. That is Hole in the Wall hideout, and is sort of our little joke because it does cover a hole in the wall. Jo Jo is back there but there is no safe. My father had no safe but made a well protected hiding place and promised Bennett he would keep the statue safe. If you would help me take the picture down please."

Behind the picture was a square of many pieces of wood. As Grace began taking the wood pieces out she explained. "Behind this wall is a square vault. That vault is walled on the top, the bottom and three sides with two foot thick adobe blocks. The only side that is not covered is this entrance and this entrance is a puzzle. If you do not take the puzzle apart properly, a forth block of adobe falls into place locking the contents inside. You would then have to tear down the whole house to get to that vault."

She finished removing the puzzle and reached inside, pulling out a package wrapped in fabric. As she unwrapped it she revealed the gorgeous little statue, thousands of years old, and set it on the table. An athletic young Minoan woman had grabbed the horns of an oncoming bull and was in the process of leaping over the Bull's head onto the bull's back. I wasn't sure what metal it was, perhaps bronze, but it gleamed like gold.

As we all sat admiring it, she said, "Sometimes on a Sunday afternoon we would take Jo Jo out and let her decorate the table as we had our dinner. We have enjoyed her company, and as you can see, we have kept her safe for the day Bennett would return for her.

CHAPTER THIRTEEN

Sam Dehany found his thighs had gone to sleep and his back hurt like hell. He had to use his hands and arms to help push himself up from the narrow aircraft seat and then couldn't move out into the aisle because it had filled with people. He stood bent over with his head bumping on the overhead luggage compartment, a position that didn't help the sharp stabbing pain in his lower back. During the flight he had tried to walk laps around the plane to ease the discomfort, but the thirteen and a half hour trip from LAX to Istanbul had been miserable. "God damned plane trip never used to hurt this much," he mumbled.

A grey-haired woman in the aisle in front of him smiled and said, "And we didn't used to be this old."

He started to give her an angry look, but realized he'd been caught talking to himself, and the look changed to a sheepish grin. "Guess I can't argue with that."

He wondered, however, just how old she thought he was, and just how old did he feel. He had turned totally grey over the last five years, though he was proud that he still had a very full head of curly grey hair, no wrinkles, and a face many woman found appealing. He was only fifty-two. He shouldn't be this crippled up by a plane trip. *More exercise, less food,* he vowed to himself.

The woman allowed a space to open in front of her so Sam could step into the aisle and retrieve his bag from the overhead. He turned to her and smiled. "Thanks," he said, then followed the crowd off the plane, down the jetway and through the modern Ataturk International Airport.

As soon as he cleared security he could see the Backpackers Travel Agency driver holding a sign with Sam Dehany printed on it. He felt almost nude entering Istanbul under his real name. He had been here many times, but always on a job that required an alias. This crossroads between East and West had always been the seat of intrigue, under the Greeks, the Romans, the Ottomans, and now the modern state of Turkey. One of the old timers Sam had trained under told him that during World War II you couldn't toss a rock in any direction without hitting an espionage agent from one country or another. Most of them knew each other, and they all lived in Istanbul like a large dysfunctional family.

The polite young driver took Sam's small bag and led the way to a minivan.

"Where to, sir?"

"The Crown Plaza Hotel, please."

"Which one?

"The one in the Sultanahmet district, please.

"Ah, nice choice. Pleasant hotel, wonderful buffet, and right in the heart of the old district. Are you here on business or pleasure?"

Absorbed in his own thoughts, Sam didn't hear or answer the driver's question. Taking his cue from his passenger, the driver settled in for a quiet ride to town.

The fourteen mile drive into town skirted along the edge of the Marmora Sea. Sam watched out the window seeing a modern freeway filled with new cars and along both sides were modern Western style buildings including sparkling glass skyscrapers. It could have been any city. "The world has become too damned homogenized," muttered Sam.

His driver eyed him in the review mirror, "I'm sorry, sir, what was that? Is there something I can help you find in Istanbul?"

Sam realized he had been talking to himself again, a casualty of those who spend too much time alone. As he looked up at the driver's eyes in the mirror, his neck popped painfully, reminding him that he was dead tired and his whole body ached. With that thought, he suddenly recalled a wonderful old Turkish bath he used to frequent anytime he could get to Istanbul. "Yes, driver, do you know if the Cemberlitas Hamam is still in business?"

With a laugh he answered, "It's been there since the sixteenth century, sir. I don't think it's likely to go out of business."

"Okay, could you please wait for me while I register and drop off my bag, then take me to the Haman?"

"Yes, of course."

"Great!" Invigorated by just the thought of the body renewing luxury ahead of him, Sam's mood began to shift. He opened his window and drew in a deep breath of moist soft sea air that filled the car with its own distinctive aroma.

As the driver turned inland and headed for the Crowne Plaza they were entering the Sultanahmet, the old section of Istanbul, which to Sam was the *real* Istanbul, where the city's true character came to life. Sam's memory drifted back to his younger days in this place, to casework that wound its way though buildings and streets that were hundreds of years old.

There was the Topkapi Palace, built in 1459 by Sultan

Mehmed II, home of the Ottoman sultans for 400 years, with
hundreds of rooms for concubines, children and servants. In Sam's
memory, however, it was the place of death for friend and fellow spy,
Davis Notts.

The Hagia Sophia with its large flat dome built in the 6th
century was an engineering marvel that still amazed Architects today.
Built by Emperor Justinian on the site of the Greek Byzantium's
acropolis, the Hagia Sophia was the largest church in the world until
St Peter's Basilica was built in Rome a thousand years later. But it
wasn't the engineering that Sam remembered. The Hagia Sophia was
where Sam met his own Sophia. As he remembered her beauty, he
tried to remember her real name. It might have been Agatha. Didn't
matter. It was possible he never even knew her real name. She had
always been Sophia to him. He wondered what had happened to her.
Was she still alive? Still a Russian agent? Maybe retired and a fat old
mama with grown children.

Then of course there was the great grey Sultan Ahmed
Mosque begun in 1609 under the rule of Ahmed I and now known by
tourists as the Blue Mosque. Sam had killed a man there, a double
agent flying under the color of the British flag, but caught out in his
Red underwear.

Sam also remembered running for his life through the great
gloomy Basilica Cisterns. They had been built in the 6th century and
long ago were used to store water for the nearby palace. He thought
he remembered seeing the cistern in an old Bond film.

Sam smiled. He had just managed to connect his life to a
Bond film. Those had not been pleasant experiences at the time, but
their memory had reminded him that he had lived quite a life. It
served to pick up his spirits and make him glad that he had decided to

investigate Eddie Hunter's kidnaping himself. Despite the debilitating plane ride, he was glad something had forced him to climb out of his hermit existence, leave his San Pedro bungalow, and come once more to Istanbul.

He pulled out his cell phone and dialed an Istanbul number he had dug out of a government data base before he left home. When a woman answered, Sam said, "Steve Crain, please. Tell him it's Sam Dehany calling."

Some moments passed before a tired male voice answered, "Look, if you jerk-offs don't have anything better to do than make prank phone calls, I'm sure I can find a pile of files to send down there."

Sam was silent a moment The voice sounded like his old friend but the greeting wasn't exactly the response he had expected.

"Steve? Steve Crain? It's Sam Dehany."

"Yeah, right. You guys obviously need some retraining. Didn't any of you dumb shits consider the fact that this call would show up as coming from an inside line?"

Sam smiled. No doubt about it. That was Steve on the other end of the phone. Sam spoke his next few words in Arabic, words he and Steve had shared many years before.

This time it was Steve who required a moment of silence, then he answered the code phrase in Arabic. When Sam countered with the correct response, Steve said, "I'll be damned. Sam Dehany. I thought they kicked you out on a section eight. What the hell are you doing in my building?"

"I'm not. My call just got transferred from another department."

"Oh. Maybe I'm the one ready for retraining. Where the hell

are you?"

"I just got off the plane and am heading for the Cemberlitas Hamam to take a cure for a thirteen hour flight. You free to join me?"

"Absolutely. See you in about thirty minutes."

CHAPTER FOURTEEN

Sam entered the high ceilinged building with its traditional domed roof which had stood on this spot since 1584. The air was moist and carried the distinctive smell of cistern water, human bodies, and soap. The light was dim, and though there were few bathers at this hour, a few words of conversation echoed faintly off the dome. Sam took a deep cleansing breath and surveyed the Hamam with pleasure. The Turkish bath was rooted in a culture of leisure and cleanliness at the height of the Ottoman Empire.

Before receiving a bath and massage Sam stripped, wrapped himself in a Turkish towel and began the restorative treatment in the warm room where hot dry air flowed over him. The room was almost empty. As the warmth of the room seeped into his body, the sweat began to trickle out and his aching muscles started to relax. His last conscious thought was, what a wonderful civilized custom the Turkish bath is.

The next thing he knew, Steve was shaking him awake and speaking in a quiet but urgent voice. "Holy shit, man! I thought you must be dead. I couldn't believe you'd be stupid enough to fall that sound asleep in an Istanbul Hamam. What kind of spy are you?"

Sam sat up lazily, still lulled and relaxed by the sauna. He smiled and took a good look at his old friend. Steve had not put on an ounce of fat, but was no longer the bean-pole youth he had once been.

He was muscular, with the body of a mature man. He was about forty-five years old, seven years younger than Sam, and though he still had a full head of hair, it was now greying at the temples. Sam smiled at his old friend and comrade and answered, "A retired one, and I would say it's about time for you to consider that life style change. You're a wee bit uptight."

Sam put out his hand for a shake but Steve gave him a bear hug instead. "It's really great to see you," said Steve. "I heard you were out, and not a word after that. Where you been?"

"I live in a comfy little California bungalow in San Pedro and spend at least half my time on my fishing boat."

"I don't believe it. Don't tell that to the young bucks who work for me. They consider you almost mythical. When they heard I was going to see you, they even tried to tail me so they could meet the great Sam Dehany."

"Where in the hell did they get that sort of image of me?"

Steve look chagrined. "I may have used a few tales from the old days in my training sessions."

Sam saw movement at the entrance to the room behind Steve's back and smiled. "They tried to tail you huh? You lose them?"

"Oh yeah. They're young and green."

"Then those two young lads who just came into the sauna room in street clothes wouldn't be your boys?"

Steve whipped around. "Oh crap. James, Alfred, what the hell are you doing here?"

James, the taller of the two, shrugged. "We just wanted to meet Dehany. We've certainly heard enough about him."

Sam leaned over and spoke quietly in Steve's ear. "Maybe

that would be a good idea. If they've got some time on their hands, maybe they could help me with a small problem."

Steve looked at them a moment. They were both in their early twenties, both smart and always ready to try any action that came along. James was the taller of the two, dark brown hair, brown eyes, not handsome, but with the self-assured composure that got the girls anyway. He was defiantly the ring leader of the two. Albert had sandy blond hair, blue eyes and a better physique that James, but he was the cautious type who would think twice and act once.

Steve asked, "James, what's that in your hand?"

With a self-satisfied grin, James answered, "A GPS tracker."

Steve closed his eyes a moment, shook his head and said, "Go get into towels. You might as well join us."

As James and Alfred headed for the changing room Steve said, "I used some of the best trade craft from twenty years in the business and lost those two in just four blocks. But I forgot about the GPS locator on my cell phone. Maybe you're right. Maybe it's time for me to retire."

After their sauna, the four of them received a traditional scrubbing, massage, and a bit of manipulating that in the U.S. might require a chiropractic license. Since other bathers were now coming in, their conversation became limited and banal, avoiding anything that might touch on their business.

Dressed and feeling totally revived and rejuvenated, Sam said, "I have a little problem I would like to get some help on. How 'bout we have dinner in my room at the Crowne Plaza where we can talk freely?"

All three accepted readily.

The Crowne Plaza was a five star hotel and the meal was a

delightful combination of Eastern and Western dishes. As they ate, Sam began to tell Steve, James and Alfred why he was in Istanbul.

"I have to tell you fellas that I am retired and what I am doing here is personal and in no way official, so if you agree to help me, there's no sanction for anything we do. Now I don't think we will be doing anything to get in trouble, but, watch yourselves. Okay?"

They each nodded.

"A little over a month ago Eddie Hunter, a good friend of mine who's a consulting mining engineer, received a wire asking him to check out an iron ore property here in Turkey. That turned out to be just a lure to get him here and kidnap him. He was vacationing at the time with his fiancé, Abbie Winter, and they decided to add Istanbul to the holiday. The kidnappers grabbed them both, beat the shit out of Eddie and threatened to kill Abbie, all in an attempt to get some information Eddie didn't even have. They finally decided Eddie's daughter, Diana Hunter, was the person they needed instead of Eddie. They searched the world for her, but she was totally off the grid and they got nowhere. In order to smoke her out, they created false death documents for Eddie and sent a sealed coffin to Diana's home town figuring she would have to surface. Once Diana arrived, they sent her and Abbie off on a treasure hunt to find some items they believe should be theirs. They're holding Eddie until the girls find the items they want, but I believe that as soon as they get the items they'll kill Eddie anyway."

Steve nodded. "We'll help anyway we can Sam. What do you need?"

"So far their actions have defeated every attempt I've made to profile and identify them. Their MO is just too weird. I mean, these guys don't operate like normal kidnapers. They seem to treat this thing like kids playing a video game or something. The only trouble is, their *play* is so vicious, I have no doubt that they could be deadly to my friends. I'm here to see if I can pick up a lead on these guys before things go that far. I could use help with the leg work if you guys have time."

Steve looked across the table at his two young trainees who were trying to put on their professional faces and not look like kids on Christmas morning.

James looked to his boss. "How 'bout it, Steve. Can we take some time off from digitizing old files?"

"I think I can spare you for a couple of days," he answered. "Log it in as professional development days." Steve smiled as he saw the delight on the faces of his young agents. It was a chance to work for the legend.

CHAPTER FIFTEEN

Sam and Steve settled into comfortable chairs in the hotel
lobby and ordered after-dinner drinks while James and Alfred started
basic legwork. The young investigators asked around until they found
the clerk who had been on duty when Abbie was taken from the hotel.
As they began to question him, Sam and Steve moved in behind them
to hear what the fellow had to say. The desk clerk's first response was
as expected.

"I'm sorry, sir, but information on our guests is confidential."

"But this woman was drugged and taken out of your hotel
against her will," said Alfred.

Haughty and indignant the clerk answered, "Where do you get
such a story? I have heard no such thing, and you don't look like
you're with the police. In fact you look very much like the young
college boys this woman left with. It was my understanding the
woman in question was here to give the boys a good time. What, do
you want your turn now?"

Steve had warned his trainees against using any official ID, so
at this point Sam stepped forward, opened his wallet on the desk and
pulled out two twenties. He left the wallet open so that an official
looking U.S. Diplomatic ID could be easily seen but not officially
presented. With calm presence and no hint of accusation, Sam said,

"Mr. Demir, I know this wasn't your fault, but I'm afraid you were deliberately misled. The woman in question is the fiancé of an American mining engineer important to American and Turkish business relationships, and she was indeed kidnaped from this hotel. The American Consulate is not interested in finding fault with the hotel, but we are very interested in finding the men who committed this crime. We would be grateful for any assistance you could give us. Now you said these were college age boys? Were they Turkish college boys?"

"No, they were American boys, and not the sort you would think of as kidnapers."

"What would you think of them?"

"The kind with more money than sense. The kind that show up here every summer season looking for mischief to get into, they kind that thinks no rules apply to them."

"Did you see them leave with her?"

The clerk reluctantly nodded an affirmative. "They took her out in a wheel-chair saying she had gotten drunk and was sleeping it off."

"Didn't you find that strange?"

Anger burned in the clerk's eyes and transformed his voice from accommodating to resentful. "When you have to deal as I do with arrogant, wealthy, influential young Americans you must learn not to find anything strange."

"I understand. I run into that in my line of work also. Do you by any chance have their names?"

"No."

"Address where they were staying?"

"No, but I heard from their driver that the night before they caused a huge fight at a dance club, refusing to pay for their drinks and their girls. Maybe the police got their names."

"Thank you. You've been a great deal of help," said Sam, and turned to leave, then turned back. "Oh, one last thing, what was the name of their driver? Maybe he could tell us where they took her from here."

"His name is Arda and he is out front right now."

Sam thanked him again, dropped another twenty on the counter, and the four of them went to speak with Arda.

Once the driver was assured that the American boys would not hear he had talked, he was glad to help. He drove the four of them out to a slum area on the outskirts of the city. The building he stopped at was a long row of worn and trashed apartments with no paint and most of the windows boarded up. He showed them which apartment the boys had taken Abbie to.

They went in though an unlocked door and found the place occupied by squatters. Three men, thin and wrapped in dirty robes lay huddled in the corners of the room. They had been asleep when Sam and his friends went in, but quickly awoke and watched the intruders with a suspicious and hostile gaze. The four men conducted a silent search of the two-room apartment and concluded there was nothing useful there. With Arda's help they questioned the squatters, but got no useful information, so the four of them loaded up in Arda's taxi.

"Arda," said Sam, "I heard that these same boys got into a fight at a local night club. Is that right?

"Yes, they had a different driver that night but he warned me about them later. They went to one of those tourist nightclubs where the owner sends beautiful girls to the young man's table. The young man buys the girls drinks which don't have alcohol, but for which he is charged a great price. The local police know this game and a few are always around to intimidate any patron who doesn't want to pay his bill."

Alfred asked, "So what happened? Did these boys refuse to pay?"

"Oh my, yes," replied Arda. "They not only refuse, they start a huge fight with the police and the nightclub employees. More special police had to come to arrest them, but of course they were released right away."

Silence followed as if Arda felt he had said all that need be said. Then James asked, "Why were they released?"

Arda looked at his passenger in the rearview mirror, not sure if the young man was ignorant or goading him. Finally he answered. "Because they make one phone call and someone powerful sees to it they were not booked. Rich young boys, no limits on their behavior."

Sam and Steve returned to the hotel to have a night cap and a long catch-up conversation. After giving James and Alfred a few instructions, Steve turned them loose to check with the nightclub and the police and see what they could learn. Steve assured Sam the boys could handle it, but like an old hen with chicks, Sam worried about what he might have gotten these young men into.

CHAPTER SIXTEEN

Our ship had been underway for more than two hours and Jo Jo now graced the table in our stateroom. I knew I would have to put her up in the safe, but couldn't resist a few hours with her. The gleaming statuette captured an iconic moment in an ancient sport. An athletic young woman faces the charge of a large horned bull. As the bull rushes towards her, she grabs the horns, vaults up and over the bull. The artist had captured the action just as the woman, holding the horns, was in the air over the bull. As I admired this priceless and unique work of art, I wondered if the ancient Minoan artist who captured this almost mythical moment in human sports ever dreamed that his bull dancer would outlive his entire civilization.

We had all showered and dressed comfortably. Though our luxury liner offered no less that eight elegant dinning rooms, we decided to order dinner in. For one thing, we wanted to be able talk freely and not have to pretend Nelson was a butler. More importantly, we were expecting a call from Dad's kidnapers and wanted to take it in the privacy of our room.

I had ordered small Mexican lobsters and they were cooked to perfection, soft and sweet without the rubbery texture often served in restaurants. Abbie had a veal dish with a delicious reduction sauce, and Nelson stuck with a well marbled steak. With excellent wines and rich desserts, we all over indulged, but we felt we had earned our victory meal this day. We had solved the first puzzle and retrieved Jo Jo.

Nelson poured us each a Kahlua and cream. "Ladies, shall we take our drinks to the veranda? It's a gorgeous clear night and the sky is filled with stars."

Abbie cast a knowing look at Nelson and then at me. With a hint of a smile she said, "You two kids enjoy the stars by yourselves. It's too cold out there for me. I'll watch a bit of tele and try to get my mind off worry about Eddie. Be sure to let me know when the call comes in."

Hmm, "You kids enjoy the stars." I didn't think Nelson and I had done anything to give away the fact that we had a romantic past, but Abbie had obviously picked up some vibes somewhere.

I slipped into my wind breaker and put my personal cell phone into my pocket. Nelson opened the slider, I grabbed a couple lap robes, and we went out to the deck chairs and snuggled down under the robes. He was right. The sky was spectacular, so many stars visible and seeming so close you could almost touch them. We sipped the Kahlua in silence, neither of us sure what topic of conversation was safe.

Finally I dived in. "I am very thankful you're here, Nelson. I understand it's because Sam asked you to help, but I want you to know I am very grateful."

"Yeah, well, thanks for hauling my ass out of the Pacific today. I owe you one."

"Ah, no. That just evens the score."

"How so?"

"Last case we worked, I seem to remember you perched on

the limb of a giant Morton Bay fig and from there launching yourself into a music room to rescue my ass from some very bad guys."

He laughed. "Oh, yes. I remember a few bruises I took for that one. Those two guys were tough." He was silent a moment and then added, "And in both instances, we had both pulled something incredibly stupid to get us into trouble. I guess we are even."

"True," I agreed. We both laughed and were silent once more. I was almost hopeful that we had made peace, but his next question and his angry tone of voice disabused me of that notion.

"Yeah, thought we made a pretty good team in more ways than one. So why the hell did you just disappear after our night in Baja? Was I a bad lay or what?"

My voice rose in anger. "Oh, for Pete sake! Leave it to a man to look for a problem in his pants. I left because I had a case, and I believe you did likewise. In fact, you were the one who got the phone call from your boss sending you off on a new job. You ended our trip to Baja, not me."

"But I asked you to come with me, to join my group and be my partner."

"Yes, and to do that I would have to give up my own PI business and be totally dependent on that mystery group of yours."

Meeting my anger he slammed his fist on the railing and almost shouted, "I should have known it! You tossed me so you could continue to play the Lone Ranger."

We were both silent, stewing in our own anger. Then I said, "Nelson, I never tossed you at all. I expected you would call and we would . . . but I got a call from an FBI agent demanding I fly out and ID a murder victim in New Mexico. One thing led to another and I ended up on a case that took me to Costa Rica. I got back from that trip to find my apartment trashed and a summons to . . . "

Whoops, almost said too much. I had to quit talking. I was getting too close to things I couldn't divulge. "So where were you all this time and why didn't you just call me?"

"Just call you? I called daily at first. Then I got back from the case the group sent me on and went to your apartment and found it trashed. I thought something terrible had happened to you. That's when I tracked down Sam and learned, no, you were just working your own case, without a word to me and not a . . ."

My cell phone rang. This was terrible. I was emotionally off balance from my confrontation with Nelson and now I had to put on the poker face and deal with the men who had Dad. Damn! I grabbed Jo Jo from the table then sat back down on the deck chair. Taking a deep breath, I handed the cell phone to Nelson and signaled him to press the button on the phone. Abbie came running out to the veranda.

Dad's image appeared on the phone and I tried to smile, tried to look calm and self assured, but Dad looked in pain. A fist slammed into his rib cage.

"Stop that," I yelled. "What's the matter with you? I have your statuette. That's our deal. Look!" I held up the statuette.

"Our deal didn't include a penthouse suite, you smart ass bitch."

"What?"

"You think I wouldn't notice? Think you'd rip me off? Well now Daddy's going to have to pay the price."

I saw his fist heading for Dad's face and I lost it. I leaped from the chair and held the statuette above the railing and over the ocean. The next words that came out of my mouth were not thought out and neither the words nor the voice even sounded like me. From somewhere deep within me there came a roar of fury.

"You fucking bastard! You touch him one more time and this little trinket is gone forever. Look at me! Look in the phone and see where I am standing. I am on the veranda and this ship is at sea. You hit my father again and I'll drop this statuette and let it sink to the bottom."

I had never been that angry and out of control. It was like I was out of my own body, standing there watching me doing things I would never do. I could hear me yelling, and part of me knew that this was probably a big mistake, but the other part of me was so enraged, nothing could stop me.

Covering his face with his hand, he peered into the phone. I looked into his brown eyes and continued to yell.

"You have made a huge mistake, my friend. You sent me Bennett's complete list of art treasures, and I am the only one in the world who can decode his notes and find the treasures. Now, if you ever want me to retrieve them for you, here's the new rules we are going to play by. Every morning at 8 o'clock I will call your number. At that time I will talk with my father and I will inspect every bit of his body. If I see one single new mark, on him I will disappear from this ship, and I will find every treasure on this list, and I will take them all to the Mariana Trench and sink them to the bottom. No one will ever find them again. You hear me?"

No answer.

"You better answer me or this little bull dancer goes into the drink. Do you understand?"

"Yes, I understand."

"Now I don't give a didly-shit about your treasures. You're

welcome to them. My father is to be kept comfortable, have good food and drink, and you're not to harm him in any way. If you keep your end of the bargain, I will bring you all your treasures and exchange them for Dad's freedom. Deal?"

No answer.

I let go of the little statuette with three fingers and was holding onto the athlete's leg by only my thumb and forefinger. I saw him gasp. "Do you agree?"

"Yes. Yes, for God,s sake bring the statue back over the deck." His phony accent had totally disappeared and was replaced by a distinctive Texas drawl.

"Good. Dad, strip." I could not resist my next dig, letting the kidnaper know that I knew. "You there, Tex, get a marking pen. I want every wound and bruise circled with the pen."

Dad looked at me with an expression that registered both shock and embarrassment. "Everything?"

"Everything. Unless, of course, there's someplace you wouldn't mind having hidden damage. Have you eaten today?"

"Yes, beans and rice with chillies."

"Not good enough. I want him to have three square meals a day, including good meats and fresh fruit and vegetables. When I call in the morning he had better be enjoying a good breakfast including plenty of hot coffee."

With that, I took the phone, clicked it off, and sank into the chair. My whole body began to shake, and I began to sob uncontrollably.

CHAPTER SEVENTEEN

It was 2:37 a.m. I had not slept. After Nelson had gotten both Abbie and me calmed down with reassurances none of us believed, he had left the cabin. His last words to me were whispered. "In case of any serious blowback, you better get out the gun Sam included in your suit case."

I put the pistol in my purse while Abbie was in the bathroom, and then sat down to try again to contact Sam. His phone went straight to voice mail. Giving up, I went to bed.

Abbie had gone to sleep a little after midnight. I tossed and turned until I couldn't stand it any longer. I dressed in jeans, shouldered my purse with the gun in it, and quietly left the stateroom. I took the elevator to the promenade deck and walked in circles around the ship. My thoughts ran in similar circles. What had I done? Would they now decide I couldn't be trusted and just kill Dad? Or would they wait until I had all the trinkets from this high stakes scavenger hunt? What had Sam learned? Could we find and rescue Dad in time? What had I done?

I pulled out my secure phone and for the third time dialed up Sam's cell. This time he answered on the first ring. "Hi Beautiful. Why aren't you asleep?"

"A lot has happened today. I had to talk with you."

"Yeah, I just got off the phone with Nelson. Hear you really cut loose on those guys. Feel better?"

"Not really. Now I'm more afraid than ever. Sam have you learned anything that will help us find Dad?

"Well, I haven't exactly got his address, but I know who we're dealing with and why. The four men who have your dad are all members of the Acclivitous Society, which is a secret college society."

"You mean like a fraternity?"

"Sort of. The senior societies only select juniors to become members in their senior year. The most famous, or perhaps infamous one, is the Skull and Bones society at Yale which has a membership that includes past presidents and senators, star athletes, top bank and Wall Street financiers, supreme court justices, heads of the CIA, cabinet secretaries, etc, etc. Every part of the WASP power structure is well salted with Skull and Bones alumni. They, however, are far from the only such society. There are, oh, I don't know, maybe fifteen to twenty of these very secret societies just at Yale."

"College boys with ties to the elite are holding my dad? Are you kidding me?"

"No, but these are not your ordinary sort of college boys. The Acclivitous Society was started in 1926 when a bright young student who appeared to have all the qualifications, like money, looks, grades, etc, was not tapped to join Skull and Bones. The one qualification he lacked was the proper WASP family connections. His daddy was an Italian. He and his Daddy got very angry when he was snubbed and Daddy just happened to be one of the most wealthy and powerful mafiosos plying the prohibition liquor trade. However, his kind of power and threats didn't hold a candle to the old money power of the Skull and Bones. So, they gave up their assault on the power elite and established a fully funded society of their own to serve their own kind."

"So why do they have Dad?"

The young CIA fellows in Istanbul who helped me with the investigation came up with two possibilities. First, one of the men who has your dad is probably the grandchild of the officer who originally stole the artwork in Germany. The fact that there are other members of the Acclivitous Society involved may indicate it's a Crooking stunt."

"And just what is a Crooking stunt?"

"Have you heard the stories of Skull and Bones stealing keepsakes from other Yale societies or being accused of having stolen the skulls of Martyn Van Buren, or Geronimo, or Pancho Villa?"

"I think so."

"Well that sort of thing is referred to as Crooking."

"And does this Crooking usually involve beating up on an old man and hiring hit men?"

"With other societies, no. But with the Acclivitous Society, it can involve much worse. No case has yet proved it, but it is believed that the Acclivitous Society can include initiations similar to the Mafia itself, where you have to kill a man to be a made man."

I had nothing to say to that, was afraid to speak. There was a long silence.

"Chin up, Diana. We'll save your dad and get these bastards. I've followed their trail to Switzerland where they stayed in the chalet belonging to one of their fathers. I know they flew back from there and entered the country at Fargo North Dakota without any passengers. They had to have Abbie and Ed stowed someplace the customs people didn't check."

"That gives me a lot of faith in our air security. Why are you so sure they had them in the plane?"

"You must be really rattled, Diana. Think. How else would they have gotten Abbie to the funeral? Now, their flight plan from there takes them to Texas. I'm on my way there now. Listen, Diana, you probably stirred the hornet's nest and you really need to be on your *cuedado*. These are kids who have never been told "no" about anything . . . their hired killers are onboard ship with you and murder is easily within their scope."

After promising to be careful, and hanging up with Sam, I continued to walk aimlessly. Everything was dark, quiet and locked up at this hour. I was about to go up to the bow when my phone rang. I jumped and answered, "Hello?" Nelson's voice was filled with panic as he asked, "Are you alright?"

"Yes, why?"

"The other private butler from the penthouse deck was shot in the head. His elevator key isn't on him."

"Oh God. Abbie's alone." I clicked off my phone and headed for the nearest stair case. Taking the stairs two at a time, I raced up toward the Penthouse deck. By the time I reached the elevator to our deck I was totally out of breath. I dug into my jean's pocket, got out my elevator key and waited, frantic with fear, while the elevator slowly descended and opened. I pushed the up button over and over until the thing finally started moving. When it stopped and began to open, I squeezed out the opening and ran across the deck to our door, I found it standing open. Drawing my gun, chambered a round, and rushed in.

The lights were off and I tried to adjust my eyes to the dark.

Then one light clicked on, the one out on the veranda. There was Abbie shivering in her nightie and with her, Archie, the largest of the two men who followed us.

I lowered my gun and held it at my side. I was in the dark entryway and I didn't think he had seen it yet. As I walked across the livingroom toward them the big bear of a man lifted Abbie by her waist and held her under his arm like a sack of potatoes.

"Hello Ms Hunter. I have a message for you. You really shouldn't play rough with these guys, because they can be a lot rougher than you."

I continued walking toward them as I watched him begin to raise Abbie up higher than the railing.

"Here's your message," he growled. "You shouldn't start dropping things because we can drop things t . . ."

Before he could finish his sentence, Abbie, now at the perfect height, kicked the underside of his chin, slamming his teeth shut and almost bitting off his tongue. Then she followed with a second kick that looked like it broke his nose. He let out a mighty howl of pain and lost his hold on her. She dropped down into one of the lounge chairs and leaped to another one to distance herself from him. He leaped up onto the first chair and grabbed her by the hair, yanking her toward him. He had some difficulty holding his balance on the lattice work of the chair, but with one hand holding her hair he slapped her in the face and pulled her closer to him and the railing.

By the time he had her tightly in his grasp I had crossed the living room and stood at the door of the veranda. I pointed the gun at his head directly between his eyes. "Set her down unharmed in the chair or you're a dead man."

At first he was startled by the sight of the gun, then he

laughed at the plastic pistol. "You gonna shoot me with a water pistol little girl." He still held Abbie's hair with his left hand but let go with the right and reached into his shoulder holster and pulled out a large automatic.

Before he could raise it and point toward me, I squeezed the trigger. His head snapped back, skull and blood spraying out to sea. His gun dropped to the deck as his body fell backward on the rail, balancing there. His left hand still held Abbie's hair in a death grip as deck chair slipped away under his weight and his body slowly tipped over the rail.

Abbie screamed as she felt his grasp yank her toward the railing. I dropped my gun and ran to the railing to grab Abbie and keep her from being pulled overboard with the killer. Suddenly Nelson appeared at my side and grabbed the killer by the arm, holding his weight while I pulled his fingers loose from Abbie's hair, one at a time. Then Nelson let go of Archie's arm, and we all looked over the railing and watched him fall nine stories into the dark night sea.

CHAPTER EIGHTEEN

In the wee hours of the morning, Nelson, Abbie and I cleaned up any splatter we could find on our veranda, but there was very little. Most of Archie's brains went straight out for fish food. We just hoped it all blew out to sea and none landed on decks below us. An early morning rain with strong winds washed the ship and gave us some relief on the matter of splatter-matter.

We also carefully bagged the gun Archie had dropped on our veranda, figuring it would probably be the murder weapon in the butler's death and would have Archie's finger prints.

Then Nelson sat me down and tried to have a psycho-babble discussion with me about the repercussions of shooting Archie. I stopped him before he got a good start.

"Hold it right there, Nelson, If you think I will have one ounce of guilt about shooting that guy, forget it. He was a hired killer, and it was clearly him or Abbie."

"Have your ever killed anyone before?"

"No, but it is well within my moral beliefs to take a life in order to save one. This will not be a problem."

"You know there's a reason that police departments offer counseling to officers who shoot in the line of duty. If . . . if later you need to talk . . . "

"Thank you, Nelson. If I run into trouble, I will ask for help. Right now however, we need to worry about other consequences resulting from this thing. Like, do you suppose anyone saw Archie fall or heard the shot."

"That's what I've been worried about," said Abbie.

Nelson said, "That concerned me earlier, but by now, not so much. It happened in the dark, late hours when everything on the ship was closed and everyone, even the party crowd was asleep. Consider the isolation of this penthouse stateroom. We are on the top deck, only one other penthouse room on this deck, and nothing but storage and garden around us. Plus it has now been several hours and no one has come knocking on our door. I think it's unlikely anyone saw Archie's swan dive."

"That was my thought," I said, "but I was afraid it was wishful thinking. Anyway, we still have to deal with his partner, Jake. Do you think we should rent another stateroom and hide Abbie so Jake thinks Archie did his job?"

"Absolutely not," said Abbie. "I'm not about to cower in a corner while you two have to deal with Jake Morgan."

Nelson shook his head. "That would mean leaving her alone."

"Well, suppose we go about our business as if nothing happened. What Jake might do is unknown, but he will certainly be mystified by Archie's disappearance, especially if Abbie and I appear around the ship, unharmed and show no signs of distress."

"That's good," said Nelson. "And while he's nonplused we'll have time to turn the investigation of the butler's murder his way. I can hide Archie's gun near the place the butler was killed, someplace I can be sure it will be found. We know from Sam that the FBI want's Archie as a suspect in several murders. Once the investigators find

Archie's prints on the gun they'll go looking for him and that will lead them to Jake who is also wanted. We can't be sure ballistics will match Archie's pistol to the slug in the butler, but if not they can check out Jake for a weapon."

I looked at my watch. It was 7:30 a.m. "I don't think there is much more we can do with this thing now. You guys get some sleep. Nelson, you better sleep here in the extra bed, for your protection and ours. I'll stay up until eight so I can call Dad's kidnappers on schedule. I won't say a word about Abbie and they won't dare ask. Just let them wonder. Then I'll get some shut-eye too. We can tackle our problems again this afternoon.

We had three days at sea before we reached our next port of call in Puerto Caldera, Costa Rica, and with the events of the last two days, all three of us needed the downtime. So, after we woke up that afternoon, Abbie and I did the only thing a woman could do under such circumstances. We hit the dress shop and treated ourselves to knockout evening dresses. Mine was a soft beige chiffon, floor length with a sweetheart neckline, form fitting to the knees and flared out from there. Our sales girl called it a mermaid/trumpet style. It came with a chiffon wrap that was a short, sheer jacket with elbow length sleeves. Abbie's was a lovely rose-red chiffon A-line that lit up her coloring and gave her a glow. It had an elegant softly draped cowl that created a modest oval neckline in front, then dropped down to the waist in back revealing a shocking bare back. It was Abbie to a tee. Diminutive and lady-like one moment and able to use either hands or feet to knock a guy's teeth out the next. When we first met she told me she would have to tell me what she was doing when she was my age. Having now seen her in action, I was sure that whatever she had done, it included some martial arts training. Fascinating! I would have to ask her to tell me.

We took leisurely baths in our sea-view Jacuzzi and did each other's hair and make-up like we were having a high-school sleep-over. We also informed Nelson he had to get a tux and escort us to the Captain's dinner that night.

By five o'clock Abbie and I, dressed, coiffed and made up, were sitting on bar stools at the main bar and saving a stool between us for Nelson. Abbie was still nursing her first Gibson and I was trying to slow down and make my second Grants-on-the-rocks last. The bar was a large circular room which sat high on the ship and had windows providing a delightful view of the sea. A pianist played accompaniment for a thin young man who did a pretty good imitation of Frank Sinatra.

A little after five, Jake poked his head through the door of the bar, squinted into the darkened room and searched from table to table. I doubted he was looking for us. He was probably searching the ship, trying to figure out what became of Archie. He spotted me, then looked quickly away and left the bar. As he went by the bar window, he took a second look my way and spotted Abbie. He could not conceal the shock and stared open mouthed for several seconds. Then he turned and walked rapidly down the deck. He did look a tad concerned.

While I watched Jake out of the corner of my eye, I was vaguely aware that someone sat down on the bar stool to my left, but was too preoccupied with Jake to pay much attention. When I turned back to the bar to pick up my scotch, I noticed my evening bag was not where I had left it in front of me, but was much closer to the gentleman who sat beside me ordering drinks. His head was turned away from me toward the bartender. I pulled the bag back, opened it, and checked all the contents. One ID, one credit card, my cell phone, a couple hundred dollars in twenties, a small mirror, comb and lipstick, my small tacky note pad and a pen, all in place. I decided I was overly suspicious. The fellow put cash out for the bartender, picked up his drinks and headed for a table a short distance away. When he sat down and I could see his face and the face of his companion, my reaction hit full alarm. The two at the table were the same two who followed Abbie and me from the funeral, and the same two who kept the guy in Baja from following us. Who the hell were these guys and what did they want?

As I was mulling over that one, Nelson came in and took the stool we had saved for him between us. He looked like he had just stepped out of a James Bond film and was ready for the casino at Monte Carlo. Abbie and I both looked him up and down. Then Abbie rubbed up close to him. Her voice was a little like Edith Piaf anyway and she played off that by using a French accent. Her delivery, however, was pure May West as she asked seductively, "Hmm, buy you a drink fella? Or should we skip the foreplay and go straight to the room?"

Nelson was speechless and the look on his face was so comical I couldn't help laughing. Finding himself the source of humor, he took a good look at both of us, dressed to the nines, picked up our empty glasses and asked, "How many of these have you ladies had already?"

"Not enough," I answered." I signaled the bartender for two more and told him to add an old fashioned for Nelson. Once we had our drinks, we moved to a quiet table off by itself to tally up the results of our day.

As we settled in to the table, I planned to tell them that the mystery duo following us had appeared again, but Nelson also had news and jumped in first. In a hushed voice he said, "I found a perfect spot for the gun. They'll find it when they do the laundry tonight. I taped it into the plastic sack to protect the fingerprints, then put it in a laundry bag with Archie's and Jake's stateroom number."

I stared at him a moment. "Oh, no. You already did it? I thought that was on tomorrow's agenda."

"Why? What's wrong with doing it today?"

"The problem is doing it at all. While you were out getting your tux I did a little computer search on how crimes onboard cruise ships are investigated. Like who's jurisdiction it is, etc. I thought I would have tonight to tell you what I've learned."

"And how are they investigated?"

"Most of the time they just aren't. The corporations that own the cruise ships register them in foreign countries, and sail under flags of convenience. About sixty percent of those headquartered in the U.S. are registered in either in the Bahamas, Panama or Liberia. None are registered in the U.S. Not only can the corporations avoid paying U. S. taxes, but their foreign countries of registration also turn a blind eye to abuse of labor laws, maritime standards, health and safety legislation, and environmental regulations. In something like, rape, disappearance, falling overboard, murder, etc. they simply claim they have no staff to investigate the complaints. They either don't report it, or report to their foreign port which does nothing. If the ship's staff gets hold of that gun, the FBI will never see the gun and never hear Archie was aboard."

"No, that can't be right," said Nelson. "I know they passed a law in 2010 that said any ship putting in at a U.S. port had to report crimes to the FBI."

"That's only if the crime is committed against a U.S. citizen. Since most ships run sweatshops with third world employees, I doubt that butler was from the states. Right?"

Nelson didn't answer, but the look on his face said it all.

"And here's another little problem," I added. "Even if we could get the gun into FBI hands, they would probably not send an investigator this far from the States. And if they did, they would run the prints, get Archie's true identity, and check out his cabin. And guess what else they might find. Both my cabin and Archie's were probably paid for on the same credit card. They might pull me into this investigation and detain me long enough to get my dad killed."

Nelson looked at his watch.

Reading his mind, I ask, "What time does the evening shift start the wash?"

"Six. Fifteen minutes. I'll never have time to change into work clothes and get down there."

"You have your employee badge and elevator key?"

"Yes"

"Then let's just go."

"In a tux? How do I explain that?"

"Come on," I said getting up. "I'll think of something on the way."

CHAPTER NINETEEN

As we walked down the deck toward the employees elevator, I stripped off the little sheer jacket that went with my dress. It was chiffon and wadded up very small.

"Here," I said. "Stuff this into your vest and tell anyone who asks that my wrap was accidently sent to the laundry and I've insisted you retrieve it for me in time for the Captain's dinner."

Nelson shrugged and stuffed it in his vest. As we reached the elevator, he used his key and all three of us stepped in. He held the door and said, "Oh, no. No passengers are allowed on employee decks."

"If someone asks what you are up to, you're going to need me badgering you to find my jacket and also confirming that I insisted you dress and escort us to dinner. And there is no way we are leaving Abbie alone on the deck."

His mouth compressed into a flat line, but he didn't argue and just let the door close, shaking his head.

It was quiet when we got to the floor with the laundry, also steamy and smelly with human sweat and dirty clothes. Not a soul was in the room, however, we soon had company. As Nelson started searching through the laundry bin for the bag with the gun, a short man in uniform came walking into the laundry room toward us.

"What's going one here? Why are you passengers below decks?"

"Oh shit," mumbled Nelson. "That's the Head Steward, my boss."

"Mr. Langly, is that you? What are you doing with passengers down here."

Abbie and I both moved to place ourselves between the Head Steward and Nelson shielding him from view with our bodies.

Nelson spoke while continuing the search. "Mr. Romer, sir, I'm here on an errand for my ladies."

"Your ladies?"

"Yes, sir."

I stepped forward a few steps and Abbie quickly followed my lead. I put out my hand and said, "Mr.Romer, isn't it? I am Diana Hunter and this is my Aunt, Abbie Winter. You helped us get a nice penthouse room. How nice to see you again."

He took my hand reluctantly and said, "I don't know what errand you're on, but there are strict rules against passengers on this deck. I must ask that you leave immediat . . ."

"Oh, we will leave soon," I assured him, "but we had a true emergency that brought us here."

"What emergency could you possibly have in the laundry?"

"Why, my wrap, of course."

"Your wrap? What sort of wrap do you mean?"

"Why the one that goes with this dress. Isn't it beautiful? I got it at the ship's dress shop. Tragically the wrap was accidently sent to the laundry." I gave a slow twirl to give him a full view and keep his eyes on me. By now other men and women were showing up to start their evening laundry shift.

"It's a lovely dress, miss, but you really must . . ."

"I will not leave without my wrap! Look how revealing the top is." With that I bent forward and gave him the bodice view. "It would be very improper for me to appear at the Captain's table without my wrap, don't you think?"

His embarrassment and unease were so obvious that it brought a few quiet snickers from the work crew. "Fine," he said, looking frantically around for some change of subject. "Mr Langly, have you found the wrap? And what the h . . .heck are you dressed for?"

Abbie moved in close to Romer and leaned in and whispered. "I'm afraid that's my fault."

Romer tried to step back from her but was backed up against a washer. He asked, "Why would it be your fault that Mr. Langly is out of uniform?"

"I insisted on it."

Romer tried to move toward Nelson and to safer ground. I stepped in cutting off his move and said. "My aunt had a terrible fright yesterday morning in port and frankly she's been terrified to leave the stateroom since. Only when we talked Mr. Langly into accompanying us as our escort, would she agree to go to the Captain's dinner tonight."

With outrage in his voice he shouted, "No, you can not take a stateroom butler to the Captain's dinner as your escort! I absolutely forbid it"

Abbie went to tears and said, "Let me show you what happened to me." She put her hand on his rear and as she started to move it south he let out a squeal and sidestepped rapidly away from her.

I added, "And if that outrage isn't enough to prove single

ladies need an escort," I said, "I'll be happy to call my uncle Marty. He's currently fishing with the chairman of the board of this cruse line, and he will report the shameful lack of concern you have for our safety."

"Miss Hunter," called Nelson. "I found your jacket. We best hurry. We've already missed the cocktail hour. Of course, that's if I have Mr. Romer's permission to do as you Ladies have asked."

Abbie and I both started to move toward Romer who was wiping sweat from his forehead with a handkerchief. Romer turned and started toward the door of the laundry room. Calling over his shoulder he said, "By all means, Mr. Langly, watch over the safety of these . . . these, delicate flowers."

Stone-faced, we left the laundry and headed for the elevator. As soon as the door shut and the box started its climb toward the passenger decks, Abbie and I both started to laugh. Nelson looked at us and shook his head. "You two should really be ashamed of yourselves. That poor man was . . ." Before he could get the sentence out he too started to laugh.

It was almost 7 p.m and getting dark by the time we escaped the laundry room, but we had to take time to put the laundry bag with the gun up to our room before going to dinner. We were close to the second elevator that would take us up to our penthouse deck when several things happened at once.

Someone said, "Get down!" Simultaneously, a human body hit me around the waist throwing me into Abbie and both of us into Nelson. The tackle knocked us all over like bowling pins. We and our tackler landed on the deck behind a stand holding life boats. Shots rang out above our heads and bullets thudded into the bulwark behind us. Not knowing who had us, we all came out swinging, and I tried to get up. A strong hand pushed my head down and a voice with a Middle Eastern accent whispered, "Diana, stay down until we have the shooter."

Shocked by the use of my name, I signaled Abbie and Nelson and we all lay still. The evening shadows were even darker on the deck behind the life boat stand, but at this close view I had no doubt. The guy who took us down, all three of us with one tackle, was one of the two who followed Abbie and me from the funeral.

From across the deck came a yell and then the sound of a fight. Then there was a sharp whistle. The shrill whistle signal was returned by our tackler, making my ears ring. Then he leaped up and vaulted over me, Abbie and Nelson like an Olympic champion. He bent down and picked up something from the deck, then ran across to his partner. Under the light from the ship's rail, we could see the two of them pick up a man who was without doubt, Jake Morgan. The three of us stood up slowly and watched as the two men carried Jake into the elevator and disappeared behind closing doors.

We stood in silence for several moments, then Nelson asked, "Who was that masked man, Tonto?"

"That was the duo who followed Abbie and me from Dad's fake funeral, *and* who kept that masher from following us in Baja, *and* watched Abbie and me in the bar this afternoon."

"So what just happened?" asked Abbie.

"What happened was those two just kept Jake from shooting us, captured him and carried him off. The question isn't what, but why?" Who the hell are they and what do they want?"

Nelson said, "Well, I can tell you one thing they wanted, because they got it."

"What?" asked Abbie and I in unison.

"Archie's gun," said Nelson. "I dropped it when I fell and the guy who tackled us picked it up as he left. Again, the question is why?"

"The question that comes to my mind," I said, "is how in the hell could he have known there was a gun in that laundry bag? Or, did he know?"

CHAPTER TWENTY

Our ship, the *Roaming Dreamer*, was relatively small, priced at the higher end of the cruise ship scale and catered to those of means. The grand dining room was elegant but understated. No Vegas style glitz and glitter on this ship. Fitting the size of the vessel, the dining room was much smaller than typical of most cruise ships and seemed almost intimate. Quiet earth tones of browns, beige, and greens covered walls, furniture and floor. Windows were hung with white sheers floor to ceiling and tables were set with white linen, crystal and silver. A dainty silver leaf pattern was glazed along the rim of the china. Lighting was recessed along the top of the wall and supplemented with delicate wall sconces. Long tapered white candles flickered at every table. As we entered, a full orchestra was playing Glen Miller's *String of Pearls*, and many couples were swinging around the dance floor.

Despite our surprise on the penthouse deck, we made it to diner just in time for the aperitif. Our assigned table was quite close to the Captain's table and he smiled and nodded to Abbie as she walked past his table. He was handsome man, probably in his early sixties and held himself with erect, military bearing. I suspected this job as a cruise ship Captain was post retirement from the Navy, but I found it strange that he wore a Navy Admiral's uniform on this ship. He seemed to be keeping an eye on Abbie.

We had agreed there would be no discussion of our situation at dinner. Tonight's dinner was to be time away from the problems. We would tackle the unanswered questions later tonight, or maybe in the morning.

As I looked around the room, I began to notice the dress of our fellow passengers. The woman just across from me had her hair rolled on what my great Aunt used to call a *hair rat,* and the girl next to her had on an old fashioned hair net. They both wore sweaters and knee length pleated skirts, and when they got up to dance, I saw they wore saddle oxfords and bobby sox. Their dates wore uniforms, one Navy and one Army, both of World War II vintage. As I surveyed the rest of the room I realized these two couples were not the only ones who looked like they just stepped out of the 1940s. Some wore elegant gowns of the period and others uniforms and bobby sox outfits like the table next to us. Now the Captain's Navy uniform made perfect sense.

I laughed with delight and Abbie, who had also been checking out the crowd, said, "We must have gotten on a special costume cruise of some sort."

"Yes," I said, " that or a time machine. It looks like we're back in World War II. The war may have been the pits, but there has never been better music. In fact, to my biased ear, there hasn't been any real music since rock and roll took over. Listen to that big band and swing sound. How wonderful."

Abbie nodded but looked suddenly sad. "Yes, Eddie loves that music too. You were probably brain washed with it as a kid. I so wish he could be here."

She looked so sad that Nelson and I changed the subject. We

chatted quietly though the appetizer and truly did escape the problems of the day, for a few moments. All of us, however, were pulled back to a sense of alarm when a ship's officer approached our table and said, "Please pardon the interruption, but I have an important message."

We all tensed, waiting to see what new problem had followed us to dinner. Then the officer turned to Abbie and made a slight bow. "You are Mrs. Abbie Winter, correct?

"Yes," she answered hesitantly.

"Mrs. Winter, if it would not be too inconvenient to your dinner companions, the Captain would like to extend an invitation for you to join him at his table and be his dinner and dancing partner for the evening."

At first she started to demur. "Oh, I don't know, I . . ." Then she looked to Nelson and me, and with small, sly smile, she turned back to the officer. "Actually, I would be honored to join the Captain," she said. As she stood, she bent over and picked up her evening bag, then leaning toward Nelson she whispered something in his ear. Taking the officer's arm, she smiled at both of us walked to the Captain's table.

We sat quietly for a few moments and watched her join the Captain. Then our continuing silence grew into an awkward pause. I wanted to ask what she had said to him, but decided I better not. Finally, Nelson picked up the wine bottle and broke the silence with, "More wine?"

As the bottle reached my glass, it was obvious I hadn't touched my wine, so Nelson poured himself more and chugged half a glass. Wow, I thought. Whatever she said really got to him.

As if reading my mind, Nelson turned, looked me in the eyes and said, "Abbie said we should use this evening to talk to each other and work out our problems." In an accusatory tone he asked, "What the hell have you told her about us?"

"Not word one. I guess she just reads people well enough to guess we have more history than just working together."

"Do all women have that talent? I remember the night we dropped in on Maude and her evil little playmates. I was really impressed later when you told me what you had read in those guys and what *tells* you saw that allowed you to draw the conclusions you did."

"No, as I remember it, you were furious with me over that evening. Thought I was, at the least holding out on you, and perhaps in cahoots with them."

"Not after you explained. And I never really thought that. I just thought you weren't telling me everything you knew about the case . . . sort of like now . . . like finding that Minoan statuette. I had the feeling all the time you were playing me, and I'm wondering what it will be like when we get to the next port. Wondering what will you hold back there when we start the search for the next piece."

It wasn't put as a question, but it was a plea for an answer. I welcomed it because I had already decided I was tired of these indirect methods of dealing with Nelson. I nodded, acknowledging his unspoken query.

"Fair question, Nelson. Let me give you as much answer as I can. I think, I hope you will understand, and we can drop the mutual distrust."

Part of me longed for much more than trust between us. Part of me longed to be back in his arms as if nothing had separated us. But, of course, that ship had sailed. I tried to think of how I could explain that there were things I could not tell him.

"Nelson, if I were to ask you who were the men in charge of

your mysterious investigation group, how they were organized, where their information came from, who they worked for, etc, you would tell me that you could not divulge that. Right?"

It was a rhetorical question, but he nodded his assent.

"Ok, when we worked together before, there were some things, like my reading people, that I just did differently than you and expected you to understand."

He started to interrupt, but I held up my hand. "However, after working with you I realized, I also sometimes played fast and loose with my partners. I was playing a sort of con on the bad guys and I expected you to be able to keep up without explanation. I apologized for that then, and I have changed in that regard."

Again, I forestalled his rebuttal. "However, there are still things I can not tell you, and not because I don't trust you. It's like you with your investigative group. It's because I owe allegiances to other people. You understand that, don't you?"

He nodded, and I continued. "The problem with the statuette was I didn't trust you to understand. So instead of just saying I know this or that and I can't tell you how I know, I did play games with the information I had. That was a mistake, and I am sorry. From now on, I will tell you what I know, but not always how I know it. You must trust me for that. I'll start right now. There will be no search for art at either Costa Rica or Panama."

"Why not?"

"Both the climate and the failure to find a safe hiding place made Bennett decide he had to find a better place for the oil paintings. Tomorrow, I must talk to his kidnappers and somehow convince them there will be no more treasure until we get to Grand Cayman. And please don't ask me how I know."

He poured more wine and was quiet as he sipped it. "Fair enough," he said, but I heard the qualification in his voice. "That, of course, wasn't what really bothered me."

"Oh? Then what . . ."

"Was it a game our night in Baja? Remember now, you're in truth mode here. I really need to know."

It hurt that he would think I would play that sort of game, that he had no idea what really went wrong in Baja. I thought I should not have to tell him, but obviously, I did. And, oh, how I wanted him to understand.

"That night in Baja was everything wonderful that it seemed to be, no game."

"Then why did you just disappear after that. I asked you to come with me, to stay my partner and join The Group."

"Don't you see what that offer asked me to give up? I had my own PI business, my own clients, my own life, and what you offered would have required me to give up all that was *me,* and become an appendage to you. I would have been willing to share our lives and our cases, but do you remember me asking if you would come with me on my next case in Costa Rica?"

"I think so, vaguely. Did I say no?"

"No. You said yes, but before you said it, you put your hand behind your back and crossed your fingers, like some little kid on the playground."

"No, did I really?"

"You really did. I saw you in the bathroom mirror." Then I started to laugh.

"What?" What's so funny?"

"Well, since we are in truth mode here, I must confess that

when you asked me if all my clients were as high paying as Maude, I also crossed my fingers before saying, yes they were"

He too, laughed and then was quiet. A waiter brought our main course. We watched silently as he set it in place. After the waiter left neither of us picked up our forks.

I watched his face and his eyes, wondering why I cared so much and hoping, wishing, he did also.

Finally he smiled and gave a slight shrug. "Ok, so both of us had our own lives we couldn't give up." He picked up his fork. He understood, he was over being angry, but that was that. I guess it was only ego that made him ask.

Then he looked into my face and asked, "But Baja ?"

"Yeah," I said, picking up my fork, "to paraphrase Bogie in Casablanca, 'We'll always have Baja.'"

He set down his fork, took mine out of my hand, then took my hand in both of his, leaned forward and kissed me. My insides did flips. He spoke quietly, "The band is playing, *As Time Goes By.* Let's dance like Bogart and Bergman in Casablanca."

He pulled me up into his arms and walked me out onto the dance floor. "I'm not too sure Bogart and Bergman were fond of each other," I said. "Maybe we better be their characters, Rick Blaine and Ilsa Lund instead,"

"Whatever," he said. He drew me close and wrapped his arms around me. The intoxicating aromas of his hair, his aftershave, the hard firmness of his body next to mine, the delicious memories of our night in Baja, it was overwhelming and wonderful.

I pulled back so I could look at his handsome face, touch his cheek and look closely into his green eyes. Then I returned his kiss. It was true. We still had Baja.

CHAPTER TWENTY-ONE

With help from Steve and his trainees, Alfred and James, Sam had tracked the subjects from Istanbul to cabin in the Switzerland, and from Switzerland they had filed a flight plan to Dallas Texas. Their plane had cleared customs at Fargo North Dakota with no mentions of Eddie and Abbie, but Sam was sure they must have been aboard. There are places on large bodied private jets that one could hide an unconscious passenger. Knowing they were many hours ahead of him, Sam caught the first flight he could to New York and then a second flight to Dallas. What little sleep he had was in the form of cat-naps on the planes. He was exhausted. When he got to Dallas he found the kidnapers plane had never landed there. Sam had taken a motel near the airport to sleep for a few hours while Steve and his crew tried to find out what had happened to the missing flight.

When they called with information, Sam rented a car and headed out to East Texas. About 3 a.m. he drove passed the main ranch house on the highway, but he knew the airstrip was some distance away near a small adobe building of some sort. Alfred had sent him a satellite photo of it along with geographic coordinates. He continued down the highway another half mile and let himself in through a ranch gate, then drove down a dirt road until his GPS told him he was nearing the site where Alfred's satellite search placed the

adobe house and landing strip. He stopped far enough away that his
car would not be heard and parked under some cottonwood trees

    Hiking across the dry East Texas ranch, he found an
observation point on a small hill overlooking an adobe house. At the
top of the hill was an outcrop of rock that gave him cover. Before
nesting himself behind the rock, he poked the brush with a stick to
make sure the spot wasn't in use by a rattlesnake. Nothing more
threatening than a horny toad ran out of the brush. Under a full moon,
he had watched the house for hours, and when the sun rose he could
see the asphalt air strip that looked long enough to accommodate the
private jet the kidnapers had flown from Switzerland. However, there
was no plane in sight and no hanger of any sort.

    About 7 a.m. he verified that someone was in the house
because smoke curled out of the chimney. Who, how many, and
whether Eddie Hunter was there, he had yet to find out.

    Alfred and James had continued working the case and had sent
Sam a full dossier on all four of the men involved in the kidnaping. All
four were college seniors and were members of the Acclivitous
Society. They were all students at Marian Ridgeright College, a
private school that catered to the sons and daughters of the very
wealthy, but seldom enrolled anyone from *old money*. The school took
no government assistance of any kind and tolerated no government
interference in the management of the college. Though Ridgeright had
established a campus in New England that would rival any of the ivy-
league schools, it would probably never be socially accepted by the
older schools. In the eighty-five years of its existence, however,
Ridgeright had succeeded in planting people in strategic positions of
power in industry, finance, the military, and government. Students of
the ivy-league might consider themselves superior to Ridgeright

alumni, but in the halls of power, they often found themselves forced to accommodate them.

Three of the students were from Texas aristocracy. Two had family history dating back to early Prohibition crime families. Marty Adacci was the ring leader. His grand father was the one who had stolen the art pieces from the Army unit protecting them in 1945. Adacci had evidently offered to find the art and hang it in the meeting hall of the Acclivitous Society. He was committed not only to avenging the theft of *his grand father's* art work, but also accomplishing a major acquisition for his society. His stature in the Acclivitous Society was thus riding on his success or failure.

Rick Myers and Frank Caminari were his wingmen and had been all through college. In addition to the usual drunken parties, the three of them had been implicated in theft of tests, plagiarism of thesis papers, hacking of the school computers and rape of a co-ed. None of the accusations had stuck, but the school was enriched by donations from their fathers.

The only odd man of the bunch was Steffen Rossie. He was from California, seemed to be a serious student, and had not gotten into any trouble during his college years. Neither he nor his father had been in business with the mob. In fact, his father was a hair dresser and owned a small chain of hair salons in Los Angeles. Steffen had been enrolled in Ridgeright and tagged for membership in the Acclivitous Society because his grandfather had been, and still was a power to reckon with in the underworld.

Sam had been retired long enough that he had very few contacts he could call on for back-up, and none of them were in Texas. He had driven to the Adacci ranch first because it had an airfield large enough to accommodate their jet, and he had taken a guess that this

might be where the kidnapers were holding Eddie. He thought he
would see if he could find them and if he did, then figure out what the
hell he could do about it.

Smoke from the chimney wasn't going to do it. He would have
to find someway to get across the open land to the house and have a
look see. He kicked himself for not having done that under cover of
darkness. "Getting too damned old for this shit," he mumbled. "Don't
even think straight."

He was visually mapping out a way to work himself from his
rock, across to the house without being seen when his still acute
hearing brought the distant hum of a jet aircraft. He scanned the skies
and spotted a small black dot heading on a trajectory that would bring
it to the adobe. Sam watched the craft fly lower and buzz the house,
then circle around and land into the wind. After rolling to the end of
runway, the plane taxied up to the pad by the house like the pilot was
parking a car at the door. The pilot cut the engine, the passenger door
opened and stairs descended to the ground, but no one got out.

Were they coming or going? What should he do? Should he
make a move now or would that get Eddie killed. Was Eddie even
here? Then at 9:10 a.m. four men filed out of the house and quickly
boarded the plane. Three of them were young men, heavily armed with
automatic rifles and side-arms. The other one was Eddie. Sam cursed
under his breath. His inaction had just lost him the opportunity to
rescue his friend, and now the pilot was starting the jet and flying off
to who knows where. At least Eddie looked well, but how long would
he stay that way?

Furious with himself and desperate for a next move, Sam
called Steve Crain who was the only contact he had backing him up on
this thing. It did seem silly, however, to call Istanbul for help in Texas.

Steve answered with, "You find him?"

Sam uttered a sigh. "Yeah, in a manner of speaking. I sat here behind a boulder watching the house and got to watch them take off with him again in that jet of theirs. They left from an airstrip here on the ranch, so I doubt they will be filing a flight plan."

Steve was silent a while then said, "I'll get Alfred and James looking into it and see if they can find out were these guys are going. Wherever it is, you'll need back-up. You can't very well take on four guys by yourself. You'll get both you and Eddie Hunter killed. When we learn their destination, I'll meet you there. I need some action anyway."

It crossed Sam's mind that Steve had come to the same conclusion he had, that he was getting too old for this kind of action. But he was in no position to object. "Thanks Steve, but I got to warn you, these guys came out of the house heavily armed. Come to think about it, there were only three of them. The fourth may still be here, or may have been dropped off before they got here. I'll check out the adobe and see if I can find anything about where they are headed."

"Ok, watch your ass. I'll get back to you when I have news."

"Right." Sam hung up and turned toward the house. Was the fourth guy in there? If He walked up would he get shot before I had time to speak? He turned and walked back to the cottonwoods where he had parked his car. If he approached by car he had a fighting chance. Abandoning stealth, he drove rapidly up the dirt road, stopped in front of the adobe, leaped out and took a position behind the car fender. Dust raised by his tires settled out on his clothes and filled his nose.

He reached under his shirt and pulled an old .45 revolver from his waistband holster. He had picked it up from a private party at a gun show. The trick to buying a private party gun with no paper work was to go to a gun show, avoid the sales booths, and look for someone just walking around holding a gun. A quiet word, an unobserved deal in the parking lot, and the gun was yours. This one wasn't the latest or greatest but it came with a holster and box of bullets, and was all he could lay his hands on during his drive from Dallas.

He moved to the adobe wall just to one side of the door and knocked on the door with his boot. No response. He tried the door handle and found it unlocked. Pulling back the hammer of the revolver, he nudged the door open and entered gun first.

The inside of the old adobe was one large dark, windowless room. It took a few moments for his eyes to adjust from the bright desert to the darkened interior. Dangerous moments. He could make out an old wood cooking stove on one side with a small sink beside it. There was no faucet on the sink but a water bucket sat on the counter next to it. There was a fireplace and hearth on the back wall and several mats on the floor for sitting or sleeping. A rickety old table with three chairs was in the center of the room. No one was in sight.

Sam let the hammer on the revolver close carefully and replaced the gun in the holster. He worked his way methodically around the room, sorted through the few bits of clothing and papers, but found nothing to give him a clue as to where they had gone.

He was about to leave when he heard a scream coming from in back of the house. There were no windows so he went back out the front door, drawing his pistol and cocking it. He walked carefully around the corner of the house and there saw a sight he couldn't believe. In the sand a few yards from the house lay a young man. He had been stripped naked and tied spread eagle to stakes on the ground. His body had been covered in grease and what had elicited the scream was that a nearby nest of red ants had discovered him and were beginning to munch.

"Holy shit! Nice games you boys play."

The young man looked at Sam, first confused, then in a frantic cry, pleaded "Untie me, please. They left me here to die. The ants are stinging and biting, please, help me."

Shaking his head, Sam walked toward the well by the windmill.

"Don't leave me, please," screamed the young man.

Sam filled the bucket at the well with water and walked back. As he poured the water over the boys body, washing off the ants, he said, "Let me guess. I'll bet you're the one from California, Steffen, right? What happened? Didn't you play nice with the other boys?"

Steffen stared at him blankly then nodded. "They told me I'd have to kill him after we got the treasure."

"I take it you refused?"

"Hell yes! Those guys are crazy. Please untie me."

"Where did they go?"

For the first time Steffen looked at Sam with fear. "Who are you? Oh, God, you're Marty's uncle aren't you?"

"Nope. Tell me, Steffen, where did they go from here in that jet?"

"I don't know. I can't talk about them. If they did this to me for refusing, what will they do next time if I talk?"

Sam set the bucket down on the ground and stamped his boots to knock off a few ants. "If you don't talk, I leave you just like you are and there won't be a next time. Now Where did they go and when do they plan to kill Eddie?"

Overwhelmed, Steffen began to cry.

Sam wasn't sure if he was disgusted with the kid for crying or ashamed of himself for making him cry. He knelt down and knocked a couple of ants off of Steffen's face. Emotion and frustration made his tone rougher that he expected. He said, "Now stop that and listen to me! I'm one of the good guys, and I'm here to rescue Eddie Hunter and toss your sorry friends in prison. But I can't very well do that if I don't find them. Now, where the hell did they go from here, and what are their plans?"

Steffen stopped crying, looked up at Sam with desperate hope on his face and answered, "They're flying to the Grand Caymans."

"Why? What are their plans?"

Steffen swallowed and blinked away a couple tears. "The guys they had on the ship watching Diana disappeared or something. They don't answer their phones. After Marty talked to Diana this morning he didn't trust her anymore, so they all decided to go to the Grand Caymans and wait for her ship to come in and follow her. They plan to kill them all as soon as they get the art work. Now, please, please, cut me loose."

CHAPTER TWENTY-TWO

Our ship sat quietly at harbor at Puerto Caldera, Costa Rica. I had been up early, and at eight had called to check on Dad. He was quiet and a bit sullen but seemed alright. I could see no signs of further beatings and he was having a good looking breakfast. Still, I felt like there was something he was not able to say to me. Finally I asked, "Are you sure you're alright? Are the treating you well?" He answered, "I'm okay except that the sun's burning my head. I'm going to need a new hat."

I took that in, decoded it, and asked to speak with his kidnapers. One of them grumbled an answer.

"I've finished deciphering Bennett's notes," I said. The bottom line is that he left nothing here in Costa Rica or in Panama.

"If you're trying to pull a stall tactic Diana, it will cost your Dad."

"Listen to me. All he had left when he got here was four very old oil paintings. The weather here was hot and humid, Bennett knew no one here and there were no safe places for old paintings, so he decided he would have to hang on to them until he got to Grand Cayman. I think he stashed the art there."

There was a long pause during which I heard muffled conversation as if they were holding a hand over the receiver. Then a different man took the phone. "You had better be damn sure Diana. We'll wait until Grand Cayman, but if you don't turn up the art, that will be your Daddy's last port of call. You understand?"

"I'll find the art. You just make damn sure Dad is well when it's time to make the exchange." On that note I clicked off the phone.

After the call Abbie, Nelson and I sat out on the our stateroom veranda, sipping coffee in silence. Finally, Nelson spoke the question that was on all of our minds. "You think they bought it?"

I looked up at him and considered my answer. Truth or feel good lie? I studied Abbie's anxious face. To my surprise she smiled at me, a rather sad smile, but her voice was calm and sure as she said, "Spit it out, Diana. We need to deal in reality here."

I returned her weak smile and shrugged. "Alright, no, I don't think they bought it. The guy sounded very suspicious of my story that Bennett left nothing in Costa Rica or in Panama. When I pointed out that all of the remaining art work was oil on canvas and would be quickly destroyed by the heat and humidity, he almost seemed to believe me, but I'm afraid I made another mistake the last time we talked. Now he may just think I'm stalling."

Abbie asked, "What mistake?"

"When he got excited and dropped that phony accent, I picked up on his East Texas drawl. My ego got in the way and I called him Tex. Really damn foolish. It not only let him know I had one small link to his identity, but I think that made them decide to move Dad again."

Nelson asked, "Why?"

"When I asked Dad if he was alright or if he needed anything, he said he was doing fine except that the sun had burned his head and he was going to need a new hat. That was code. When I was a kid, every time we were going to have to move again Dad would say, 'Well,

Chick, I think we better go and buy a new hat.' First, he would lead me through a geographical puzzle to guess where our next *grand adventure* would take us. Then we would choose some hat that would fit the climate or regional dress of our next destination. It was his way of imbuing the move with excitement about the new place rather than regret at leaving a school or friends or whatever. Anyway, when he said he was going to need a new hat, it meant that they were about to move him.

"You know, Abbie, when Dad sent me a text at the funeral, telling me to go with you, he told me you needed a new hat. That told me two things, that we were taking a trip and that it really was Dad sending that text . . . that he was still alive."

She nodded. "So why do you blame yourself for them moving him?"

"Sam had already told us he believed they had flown to Texas. During our last call when I blew up, I called that guy Tex . . . well, I think I may have hit too close to the mark."

Nelson asked, "So do you really believe nothing is here? What do we do with ourselves for the next few days?"

"I don't know. I'm thought out. Maybe take a swim, hit the casino, take a nap, enjoy the cruse."

For lack of anything better to do we all went to the pool after breakfast and then had lunch at the pool side bar. We were back from the pool and had finished our showers when we got a call from Sam that changed all our plans.

When I saw it was Sam calling on my secure line. I answered and put it on speaker so we could all hear.

"Hi Sam. You're on speaker. Nelson, Abbie and I are all here. What's up?"

"He was quiet a moment, then said, "Well, the good news is, 'I've seen Eddie and he looked well, but . . . I screwed up. I sat on my ass in the dark waiting to see if they were in the adobe on the Adacci ranch, and when they came out, they were all heavily armed and had the plane waiting. They took off with him and I missed my chance to rescue him. I'm so sorry. "

Sam, I'm afraid their moving him is my fault, but let's skip all the *mea culpas* for now. Tell us what's happened on your end, and we have quite a bit of news for you too, some of it rather strange.

Sam gave us the brief version of his trip to Istanbul, his investigation and tracking of the gang that had Eddie from Istanbul to Switzerland to Fargo to Dallas. He paused to explain, "I couldn't have done any of this without the help of an old friend, Steve Crain, and two young men training under him. Steve and James and Alfred are all still with the company and stationed in Istanbul. They are all working with no company sanction, and I owe them a lot.

Sam then gave us the details of his surveillance there and his finding of Steffen.

"These guys who have your dad may be college students, but they are not to be considered just kids. They are shot in the ass with silver dollars and connected to the mob. Unlimited funds and no limits on what they might do. Steffen said they told him he couldn't be a life member of the Acclivitous Society until he had killed his man. When they started handing out the kill assignments Steffen decided he didn't want anymore of them. When he tried to pull out they staked him out for the ant picnic. Steffen says that as soon as they have the art, they plan to kill all of you. Don't think they know about Nelson, but certainly Diana, Abbie and Eddie."

There was a long silence as we all digested the information.

Then I said, "Thank you, Sam. Without your trip to Istanbul and your investigation, we'd be blind to all of this."

"Yeah, well, if I hadn't set on my ass in the desert, Eddie would be free now."

"No," I said. "It's more likely he and you would both be dead. You can't take on four heavily armed men alone. Where are you now and what is your next plan."

"I'm calling from the Dallas airport. Brought Steffen here. We called his father who told the kid to hop the first plane to L.A."

"Any chance Steffen might call his friends?"

"Not a chance in Hell. The kid talked to me all the way here. His dad opted out of the mob connections decades ago when he moved to California and opened his hair salon. But, Steffen's grandfather had gotten him a full ride scholarship to Marian Ridgeright and really put the pressure on him to join Acclivitous Society. This little trip was the first time he realized what he was into, and it scarred the shit out of him. I suspect he will finish his last year at UCLA. I would love to hear what "Grandpa" has to say when he hears about all this. He may have wanted to lure the boy back to the fold, but I doubt he will take kindly to Steffen's initiation."

Sam paused and added, "There is one other thing Steffen told me. Not sure how relevant it is, but Steffen says theses guys are addicted to on-line game playing. Marty is some sort of international Gamemaster on a very violent game. He spends eight to ten hours every day on the thing."

"That makes perfect sense out of what has seemed nonsense. So much of what he and his cohorts have done didn't seem to fit any kidnapper MO. The bastard has turned mine and my Dad's life into one of his games."

"I'm afraid you're right."

Nelson asked, "Any idea where they are going from Texas?"

"Yes, Steffen says they are headed for a place in Grand Cayman. Some house owned by one of the kid's parents. I've got James and Alfred searching for an address. Marty Adacci decided that since the watchers he sent your way have disappeared and you're stalling on the other art work, they will catch up with you when the ship docks and keep an eye on you personally."

"Thanks, Sam. That helps me know what to do next."

"Yeah, well be very careful. Remember, Steffen also said that once they have the art work they'll kill all of you."

I started to tell Sam what I planned, but he asked, "By the way, what happened to the thugs they had watching you?"

We were all quiet for a moment, then I answered, "That could be a long story. I'll try to keep it brief. One of them, the big beefy guy, Archie Simon, killed one of the penthouse floor butlers and used his elevator and room keys to break into our stateroom. When I got to the room he was there trying to toss Abbie over the railing into the ocean. I . . . I had to shoot him. It was him or Abbie."

Sam didn't say a word, just let me continue the story.

"We dropped him in the ocean and cleaned up the mess and hoped no one had seen or heard anything. It all happened about three in the morning, and our room is very private and isolated. There is only one other penthouse stateroom, and it is at the other end of the ship. There is a small garden and some storage rooms in-between. We saw the other thug the next day. Jake was looking around the ship like he was trying to find Archie. He was astounded to see Abbie and I alive and well in the bar. We weren't sure what he would do. Then that evening as we were on the way to dinner, a very weird thing happened.

You know those two guys who followed Abbie and me from the funeral?"

Very guarded, as if holding his breath, Sam answered, "Yes, what about them?"

"One of them, a small guy tackled me, throwing me into both Nelson and Abbie and taking us all down to the deck behind some lifeboats. When I struggled to get up he called me by name, and said 'Diana, stay down until we get the shooter.' By then bullets were thudding over out heads and into the bulwark behind us so he didn't have to say it twice. Then we heard someone yell, Jake we think, then the sound of a fight, then quiet. Then the guy who took us down got up, leaped over us, and went to his pal and the two of them carried Jake off and down the elevator. We haven't seen a sign of any of them since."

Sam was absolutely quiet.

"Sam," I asked, "do you have someone else protecting us?"

"No. Diana, did the guy who spoke to you have any accent you could identify."

"Not really, He sounded Middle-Eastern but I don't know those accents at all, so can't be more specific. You have any idea who they might be?"

"It's just a guess, but who else would be interested in Nazi-looted art?"

"Oh," I said following his thought. "Israelis? You think they might be Mossad?"

"Possibly. But then Israel has dozens of security agencies. Could be a different one dedicated to finding Nazi loot. I think your uncle worked with Israel on some of his finds. Or maybe these guys are just thieves trying to piggy-back on your discoveries. Watch yourselves and I'll see what I can find out." Steve and I are flying to the Grand

Caymans. He's going to give me a hand finding and rescuing Eddie. He's doing it without official sanction, of course, calling his trip a vacation. I'm going to owe him, big time."

"If I am right," I said, "Grand Cayman is where I will find the rest of the art work, too. Since we now know the kidnappers plan on meeting the ship, we'll arrive ahead of the ship, and have time to find the art before they expect us. Maybe we can get ahead of them this time."

CHAPTER TWENTY-THREE

I was up early and made my call to Dad's kidnapers. I could see
Dad sitting at a nice dining table eating a good breakfast and could
easily see they had moved locations.

A second call to check in with Sam got me only his voice mail
and I assumed he was en route from Texas to meet Steve in Grand
Cayman. I left him a short message, then turned to the business of the
day.

"Nelson, Abbie, please dress casually, shorts or something. We
can't know for sure who else may be watching us, so lets leave the ship
looking like we are heading for a shore excursion. No suitcases, just a
purse or bag with things you'll need over the next day or two. We'll
buy anything else we need when we get there. If we don't get back
aboard in Grand Cayman, we can have the ocean liner ship our
suitcases to us."

Nelson tilted his head to one side. "Another shopping trip in
Grand Cayman? Who's paying for all this?"

I considered reminding him that we had a no questions policy in
effect, but Abbie was standing right there listening, so I tried a bit of
guilt instead.

"I am. This's my father's life at stake. I'll cover the tab."

Properly chagrined, he said, "Sorry, just concerned about your costs."

I got out my large shoulder bag which was my airline special and was always folded up in the bottom of my suitcase. It looked like a purse so didn't get counted as luggage but was big enough to be an overnight bag. First I retrieved Jo Jo from the room wall safe and wrapped her in a one-day change of underwear and a t-shirt. Then I folded a pair of jeans around my gun and packed it on top of Jo Jo. I started to sort though all my purses and decided I didn't have time, so I just dumped in the contents of my fanny pack and my evening bag in on top of the jeans. I would have any personal item I needed, and I could buy clothes etc in George Town. I put both phones on my belt and pulled my shirt down over them. That would have to do.

"Nelson would you please arrange to have a taxi meet us at the dock in a half an hour?"

He laughed. "I'll bite. We going to the Grand Cayman by taxi or should I also try to find an airport and a flight to George Town."

"I gave him a smile, hoping our new found friendship wouldn't crash. "No, I'm sorry, I should have explained. We take the taxi to Juan Santamaria International in San Jose. A plane will pick us up there to fly us to George Town."

He gave me a sightly questioning look and asked, "When did you book the flight?"

"While you were down picking up our laundry." I knew that when we got to the airport and he saw what kind of flight I had booked there would be more questions. Maybe by then I would dream up some suitable answers.

The drive to the airport was about thirty-five miles and gave us a chance to relax and view the Costa Rican countryside. We went through a few small villages, and in some places the rain forest came right down to the road. The closer we got to town, however, the more barbed wire we saw around both businesses and private homes. I had noticed that when I was in San Jose last year and wondered about their claim of having a low crime rate. If they have so little crime, why did so many folks feel the need for high fences topped with coils of concertina wire?

When we got near the airport I directed the taxi driver to a nearby hotel. Both Nelson and Abby shot me questioning looks, but kept silent until the driver dropped us off and pulled away. Then Nelson asked, "Why are we going to a hotel? Thought you'd booked a flight."

"It's a private jet. I have a friend who owns a corporate jet and he has loaned it to me for a few days. It will take six or eight hours to get here, and then the pilots will need sleep. We will be leaving early tomorrow morning. This afternoon we can go to the mall, buy some clothes, and make plans for tomorrow."

Abbie looked worried. "That seems a terrible waste of time. Can't we get a regular scheduled plane today?"

"Maybe, but what if these guys who have Dad take off again in their jet? This gives us our own wings to follow as needed. Besides, we still have plenty of time. Those guys don't expect us until the ship gets in. Our ship will be in Puerto Caldera until nine pm tonight. Then it will be at sea for a day, then take a day making the transit of the Panama Canal, another day at sea, a day in Curacao, another day at sea. It gets in to Grand Cayman at ten the next morning. So it will be six days before they expect us. By arriving in a private plane we will get four and a half days to find the art and find my father before they even know we're in town."

Nelson shook his head. "You have a *friend* who *loaned* you his corporate jet. Nice friend to have."

His tone was sarcastic and his mood had swung back to
suspicious. I really couldn't blame him. I was lying to him again. But
there was no way I could tell him that I had inherited a fortune that
included several corporations and a Gulf Stream Jet. Keeping Bennett's
secrets depended upon keeping his fortune hidden under the layers of
corporate structures he had set up. Robert James had told me that to
expose the structure would not only endanger the work Bennett had
given his life to, but would most likely get me killed. Bennett had made
a lot of powerful enemies.

At that moment I saw so clearly why Bennett had lived all his
life without ever marrying. I saw my own bleak future and realized, no
matter how much we might be attracted to one another, Nelson and I
probably had little chance of working things out. But I had to try. I took
his hand and looked into his face. "Nelson, this is one of those places
we talked about. You just have to trust me. I will not always be able to
tell you everything."

We booked two rooms, Abbie and I staying together. I gave
Nelson a charge card to cover his wardrobe purchases, and he left on
his own saying he would see us for dinner. Abbie and I grabbed a taxi
and headed to the Mal San Pedro, bought a suitcase each, filled it with
lovely clothes, then returned to the hotel and had the valet service dry-
clean or wash and fold all our new things. For dinner I took us to a
French restaurant. Le Chandolier. I had eaten there last year and found
it memorable. This trip it was just as wonderful as I remembered. One
thing I insisted on was the Crema de Pejibaye, a cream soup made from
the palm peach. At home I had tried to recreate this heavenly soup but
mine came out so bad I threw it all away. We got back to the hotel
early, packed our suitcases and went to bed. Tomorrow would be the

beginning of our final push to rescue Dad and put some really bad boys
in jail.

As we boarded the Gulfstream GV, Abbie and Nelson got an
illustration why I asked Robert James to send the plane. Private aircraft
have separate terminals with expedited customs procedures. No
standing in long lines with hundreds of other travelers. Sometimes the
customs agents ask you to come to their offices and sometimes they
meet the plane. The flight attendant, Danny, greeted me by name and
treated me like a long lost friend. This was not lost on Nelson. I smiled
and answered, "Thank's Danny. Please tell Robert James how grateful I
am for the loan of his plane."

Danny didn't miss a beat, but smiled and said, "I certainly will
Miss Hunter." He had worked for my uncle long enough to understand
immediately. Before we took off he went into the captain's cabin and I
knew he would clue in the pilots, Bob and Sparks. Sure enough, when
Bob greeted us over the speaker, he said, "Good morning Miss Hunter.
It's nice to have you and your friends as guests this morning. Please
fasten your seat belts. We will be taking off as soon as the tower gives
us clearance."

By 6:05 a.m. we were speeding down the runway for take off.
The three of us sat in comfortable chairs around a table and were served
a delicious breakfast of eggs, ham, pastries, fruit, fruit juice and coffee,
all fresh and bought locally in Costa Rica. Danny takes great pride in
the food he serves. We kept our conversation to small talk while we ate.
Then Danny cleared away the dishes and brought each of us a laptop
and told us it was alright to use the Internet and cell phones until we
were about to land.. Exhibiting the art of discretion, Danny went to sit

in the back of the plane, put on earphones and settled into a movie. I pulled out the iPad and began my show and tell.

First, I showed them the comments on Bennett's old voyage itinerary and explained why I felt there was nothing left in either Costa Rica or Panama. Bennett found the weather hot and humid and didn't find anyone he could trust to leave the art work. Then I showed them the one comment that made me believe he had deposited the paintings in Grand Cayman.

"Here he says, 'On this lovely small isle I finally found the most delightful spot of the trip. It has perfect temperature and ideal humidity. Its owner lives on a shady, protected bluff above the north **bank**. If I didn't need to get back to New York I could stay here forever'."

They both looked at me blankly and for a moment I doubted the wisdom myself. But with nowhere else to go, I forged ahead. "You see how bank is overwritten and darker than the rest of the text. I think he found a bank with a vault that could store the paintings."

"A bank? And this is all you have to go on? Even if he did put it in a bank and you have to admit that's a real long shot, how would you get it out? The bank secrecy laws here are powerful."

"I've used Bennett's bank accounts before and I have all the documents showing I am his heir. All we need to do is find the bank and show my credentials and we will have the art."

They both just stared at me, Abbie looking dismayed and Nelson looking disgusted. "Here," I said, "I'll show you, open your laptops and go to this site and it will show you a list of banks in the Caymans." With a sideward glance at one another, Abbie and Nelson reluctantly opened their laptops and typed in the site I had written.

After a few moments reading Nelson said, "Did you by any chance notice how many there are? There are over 600 banks on the three islands that make up the Caymans. Do you really think we can check 600 banks in four days? Diana, this is nuts."

"There are 600 plus banks now, but not in 1949 when Bennett came through here. The Caymans didn't become the giant financial center it now is until the 1980s when many people were looking for tax shelters to hide their wealth. First, we narrow the list to banks that were established before 1949. Then we divide the list between us and check the services offered by each one to see which ones have a museum quality vault for storing fine art. Then we can narrow the possibilities again by checking when that vault was built. If it wasn't there in 1949 we can check it off the list. By the time we set wheels down in George Town we will have narrowed the 600 banks to maybe six."

CHAPTER TWENTY-FOUR

We spent the flight researching the banks and found that my optimism was rewarded and my prediction almost on the money. By the time we landed in this British island dependency, we had completed our research and had just five banks that met the criteria.

At Owen Roberts International Airport in George Town, we taxied up into Cayman Corporate Jet Air Terminal and were met on board by the customs officer. He already had all of our pertinent data sent to his office by the Corporation that owned the Jet. He just needed to see our passports and verify our ID.

We also had arranged for a car and driver to meet us. Abbie had offered to drive since she was used to driving on the British side of the road, but she didn't have an international driver's license, and we wanted someone who knew the island so we wouldn't waste time looking for places.

We had our driver help us find to a small motel off the beaten track and away from the major hotels. Still operating under the principle of safety in numbers, we registered for a two adjoining bedrooms so we could all stay together. Our driver, who introduced himself as Mr. Johnny, waited while we made a quick stop to register and change into business clothes. Then with high hopes, we began our search.

Nelson again posed as my attorney. We kept our story as vague as possible, but had to supply enough information for them to at least look for an account under the name Bennett Hunter. Two of the banks refused to even look until I submitted my paperwork showing that I was Bennett's heir. Two others did a cursory name search and came up with nothing. By late afternoon we had spoken to four of banks and found nothing. Near closing time, we sat at the desk of a bank clerk in the fifth and last bank on our search list.

Mr. Havershim was trying to help us, but as we went over the request for the second time he was occasionally checking his watch. He was quite young, had an educated British accent and had probably gone to a university in England, but every now and then a bit of island lilt slipped into his speech, letting me know he had been born here in the Caymans. He was very polite but after hearing *Attorney* Nelson Langly for the second time he said apologetically, "I do understand the situation, Mr. Langly and Miss Hunter, but as I explained, your documents, though they look most genuine, must be verified. If it were up to me I would approve your application at once, but unfortunately it is not up to me. Our rules are absolute and unshakable. Your documents must be checked and verified before I can do anything. I can't even tell you if there is or is not an account in the name of Bennett Hunter until that is completed. Now that will only take about three days. We have excellent telecommunications here and most of this can be quite quickly verified."

Though he said he could not verify if there was an account, he was not much of a poker player. His expression as he had searched the computer data base made me believe there was an account. However, if we had to wait three days to access it, it might be too late to ransom my father. He saw from the looks on our faces that this was not the answer we were looking for.

"I'll tell you what. I will stay after closing this evening and get
started sending off your documents for verification. He looked at our
faces. Then to my amazement, he reached inside his suit coat and
pulled out his wallet. "I'm not sure I understand why this matter is so
urgent, but if a short term loan would help, I could . . ."

I smiled at his concern and generosity and tried to imagine any
bank clerk at home making such an offer. "No, Mr. Havershim. Thank
you. You are very kind, but that's not necessary."

"Then I am afraid there is nothing else I can do for you today. I
am sorry."

"You know," I said, "there is one other thing I might ask of you.
I realize you can't reveal whether or not there is an account under the
name of Bennett Hunter, but could you please do this. If,
hypothetically, there was such an account, could you check and see if
there are thumb prints on file for immediate identification of the
account holders."

"Thumb prints?"

"Yes, do you use those little gadgets that can read a print and
identify account holders. I know that Bennett used such a device in at
least one other bank and included a file of my print as a second account
holder."

I saw Nelson's eyebrows rise at the mention of another Bennett
bank account. He was learning way too much on this trip, but there was
no cure for that.

"Yes, yes, I know what you mean," said Mr. Havershim.
"Please just wait one moment." He rose from his desk and went to
confer with someone in an inner office. He was gone more than fifteen
minutes but when he returned he had a broad grin and was holding a

small device like the one I had used in a German bank when I accessed Bennett's account there.

"So sorry I didn't think of this before, Miss Hunter, but here at Cayman First Savings, we seldom use this device."

He quickly checked my print, compared my identity to the bank records and smiled broadly. "Yes, Miss Diana Hunter. You are indeed a legal account holder. But . . . we close in five minutes. Can you obtain what you need from the security box in that time?"

"Security box? Doesn't this account have a deposit in your, your, what do you call it? Your vault that has temperature and humidity control?"

He was silent a moment as confusion played on his features. His young face took on a look that was totally crestfallen. "If you mean like a museum vault, we have no such vault anymore. Have not had in decades. When the original owner of Cayman's First retired, there were only a few items in that vault and the new president didn't want the expense of maintaining it, so, it was taken out." He looked at our faces which I am sure registered our disappointment. After a pause he inquired, "Would you still like to look into the security box?"

I checked out the box and found a gun, cash in British pounds and U. S. Dollars, and a few passports for Bennett under different names. In the days before international ATMs and bank account withdrawal cards, Bennett had made a habit of stashing cash in deposit boxes all over the world. When possible he also left guns and passports. There was no art work and no information to help us find the art. I examined the gun, a Walther that looked as if it must have been in there since 1949. It had been rusted by accumulated moisture in the security box and would need to be cleaned and oiled and possibly even reblued, before it would be safe to use. There were no bullets for it anyway.

As our driver took us back to our motel no one said a word. At the motel I paid, Mr. Johnny and tipped him liberally. He had been helpful, efficient, and full of interesting information about the island. One thing he had explained was why he and so many other islanders we met that day, introduced themselves by their given names, like his *Mr. Johnny*.

"Here in the Cayman Islands," he explained, "we have so many people with the same surnames that it is sometimes easier and less confusing to use our given names." He didn't need to explain that courtesy was highly valued. Everywhere we went we observed the great politeness with which the islanders treated everyone. It made the common curtness of tourists shout out like they were using a bullhorn, yet most of them didn't seem to hear themselves.

"Thank you for all your assistance, Mr. Johnny. Would you be available to pick us up tomorrow morning at half past eight?"

"It would be my pleasure, Miss Diana."

I had no idea what we would do the next day but figured we might as well get an early start on doing something.

On the outside chance we might be spotted by Dad's kidnappers we decided to eat in. Nelson went out to a neighborhood restaurant and brought back dinner. He came back with a large box filled with covered Styrofoam plates and paper cups, as well as sacks of food and plastic utensils.

"It smells delicious. What is it," I asked as he set it out on the table.

"I got several things so we could sample local cuisine. Everyone try a bit of everything. This is green turtle soup," he said while setting out the paper cups. "These little fried things are conch fritters. They're good, I tried one walking back. Here, Diana, thought you would like this, butter rum lobster. Got three of them so we can all try them. These veggies, the woman called, *breadkind*. I asked her what that was and she said, casava, papaya and yams.

"Looks wonderful Nelson. I vote you do the food run more often."

Then with a flourish he pulled out a bottle. "I also bought a bottle of Tortuga rum and rum punch mix. Thought we could all use a drink this evening."

"You're absolutely brilliant, Nelson."

He used the bathroom glasses and mixed us all a large drink, and we *tinked* glasses like we had something to celebrate.

However, as we ate we were almost as quiet as we had been in the taxi, everyone knowing my one and only idea had failed and no one wanting to say it out loud. None of us wanted to face the question of where do we go from here. After dinner Abbie and I did KP by simply loading everything back in the box and taking it out to the trash. Then we all showered and went to bed early, too depressed to think about what we would do in the morning.

I was awakened at a little after seven by Nelson pounding on our bedroom door and announcing he had a pot of coffee and some rolls. When we didn't roll out of the sack sufficiently fast, he came in our room and shook both Abbie and me. Then with a finger to his lips entreating silence, he held up a piece of paper saying: "We have company, and I think we are bugged."

Nelson went back into his room and Abbie and I dressed quickly. When we came out he pulled a tiny slit open in the curtain and pointed out. We each peeked out. I was astounded to see one of our two mystery men. They had followed us from the funeral and followed us into Cabo, and tackled us on the deck of the ship. But how could they possibly have followed us here? What's more he seemed to want us to see him. He was just sitting in a chair on the patio by the pool, reading a magazine. I looked at Nelson, dumbfounded.

We all sat down at the table and I took a notepad and wrote, "They couldn't have followed us, they must be tracking us, phone GPS?"

Nelson shook his head and wrote, "1) can't track the secure phones Sam gave us and 2) they can *hear* us as well as follow us."

Abbie wrote, "How do you know they hear us?"

Nelson took the pad and answered, "When they tackled us on the ship, that guy had to have known the gun was in the laundry bag, so whatever they are using had to be on us that evening. What did we have then that we brought with us? All our evening cloths, even the shoes were left on the ship?"

I knew immediately. I wrote, "Things in my evening bag. One of those guys sat beside me at the bar and I thought he had taken something, but maybe he left something instead."

When I packed to come to George Town, I hadn't taken time to sort through my various purses but just dumped everything from the fanny pack and my evening bag into my shoulder bag.

I got my shoulder bag. I had left Jo Jo and my gun in my suitcase as I didn't want to carry them around the island. I dumped everything else out in the middle of the table.

We made small talk about the food, the weather, etc as we sorted through the stuff and I tried to remember what things had been in the evening bag. My ID and one credit card which I had returned to my wallet. I pulled them out and put them in a separate pile. There had been my cell phone and a couple hundred dollars in cash. I put the cell in the small pile and Nelson began checking it for bugs. There was also a mirror, comb and lipstick. I set those in the pile. What else?

Abbie was nervously tapping the pen we were using against the pad. The rhythmic thumping was distracting my concentration. Then it dawned on me that was the answer. The pen. I always carry a small notepad and a pen for any notation I might need later. That night I had a small tacky note pad and a pen. I dug through the stuff from my purse and came up with three pens.

Nelson pulled the first one apart and found just a pen, then he took the second one apart and found both a tracking device and a listening device. The three of us looked from the electronic gadgets on the table to each other, to the window. What should we do?

I wrote, "Let's leave it. I don't think they mean us any harm and they have helped us twice, once in Cabo and once on the ship."

Nelson wrote, "But what do they want?"

I answered, "Since the art is Nazi loot, my best guess is that they're Israeli following us to recover the stolen art."

Abbie wrote, "What happens when we find the art?"

I shrugged and wrote "They can hear us. They know what we are doing and why. Also, they want us to know they're here. These guys are way too good at their job to sit in plain sight unless they wanted to let us know. So far they have been more guardian angels than opposition. We may need their help again."

We all looked at one another in doubt, not knowing for sure if this was a safe gamble. Finally, Nelson nodded and Abbie shrugged a hesitant acceptance. Nelson put the pen with the listening and tracking devices back together and handed it to me to return to my purse.

I pointed to my watch. It was almost eight and time to check up on my Dad and call Sam. I sat on the floor in front of the draperies so they couldn't see where we were. The men who held Dad didn't even speak to me, just turned the phone revealing Dad, ready for inspection. I knew when we rescued him I would catch hell for this routine, but once I had demanded it, I had to stick by it. I checked out his bruises and saw most were fading and he had a bit of a tan. He sat back down to his breakfast which looked good, and the phone clicked off.

I called Sam and he picked up before the first ring finished. "Hi, Diana," he said in almost a whisper. "Can't talk. But we are in George Town. Later."

CHAPTER TWENTY-FIVE

Sam Dehany and Steve Crain sat in a small boat off the West Bay shore north of George Town. Fishing poles lay against the gunwale with fishing lines dangling into the water. Though small binoculars, they surveyed a three story house perched on the edge of the bay.

It was painted a rather unpleasant mustard yellow with white trim. Attached to the left side of the home was a boathouse which held a large inboard speedboat. Steps rose from the boat house offering access to the first floor of the house, then a curving stairwell accessed the second floor. On the roof of the boathouse was a sun deck with potted palms, tables and deck chairs, a BBQ, and a bar, all neatly encircled by a rod-iron fence. Outdoor decks circled the house on both the first and second floor and there was a small deck on just the front center of the third floor. Rooms on all three floors had huge picture windows with views both landward and out to sea. To the right side of the house was a small, unattached garage. Riprap lined the bank in front of the house to armor the shoreline against high tides and storms.

Steve finished his survey of the place and handed the binoculars back to Sam. "What do you think? Are they there?"

"Yeah, I think they're there. It's early. Diana probably just woke them up when she called to talk to her dad. We'll probably start to see some movement soon."

"How long you figure we can *fish* out here without raising suspicion?

"Probably not long. That whole place is windows and outdoor living space. We might as well be trolling in their living room."

"So, what's the plan, Sam? We spot Eddie Hunter and call the local police or just try to grab him ourselves?"

"I been worrying that one all morning. If we try to grab him, we have to make damn sure we do it in a way that won't get him killed. But, we really don't have anything to take to the Royal Cayman Island Police but a tall tale. Once we have Eddie, he could make a complaint of kidnaping, but I'm not sure what the hell they'd do with that. The alleged kidnaping took place in Turkey and both the victim and the kidnapers are American citizens. The Cayman police probably won't touch it, and who the hell else we gonna call for help? Even if you or I could call on an old company contact, they'd have no cause for legal action here and trying to get help for a black ops would take longer than we have. Even if we had time and opportunity to develop a legal case against these guys, it would have to be a U.S. case and I don't think the Caymans have an extradition treaty with the U.S."

"Well they're a British dependancy. Wouldn't they be covered by our treaty with the United Kingdom?

"I don't know, but what the hell does it matter? Developing a case against these guys, would take months or years, and the bastards wouldn't even be here then. None of that helps rescue Eddie right now. The only thing I know for sure is that I don't want to sit here on my butt again and let them move him or kill him while I do nothing."

"Well then, I guess the plan is to grab Eddie by ourselves in a way that doesn't get him or us killed, and to worry about nailing the college boys later. Right?"

"Right," answered Sam, now sitting up and looking intently at the house. "Here we go. I see Eddie coming out on the sun deck with one guard. So we know he's here. He looks well enough. The guard has one pistol stuck in his waist band, and a drink in is hand. I don't see the automatic rifles they had in Texas."

"I doubt they could have brought them through customs here. They probably had to leave them on their private plane back at the airport."

"How you suppose they got the pistol?"

"Well this house belongs to the Caminari family. I'm sure they found someway to smuggle some guns in here."

James looked though the binoculars. "That kid guarding Eddie is Frank Caminari, and he's walking to the rail for a look our way. Let's troll on up the coast a bit."

They hauled in the fishing lines, stowed the poles, and Sam started the outboard. Once out of sight of the house returned to the marina at high speed. Sam yelled over the noise of the motor and the water, "As soon as we get back to the marina, I'll turn in this little boat and make arrangements for a small cabin cruiser for this afternoon. We can tie up at that public dock just up the bay from the Caminari house."

Steve nodded and finished the thought. "Good. We can keep an eye on things without being seen"

Sam added, "We'll hit the place after dark. It's wide open. We'll have surprise on our side and they're just three green kids. We can handle this."

Steve laughed. "Yeah. Three green kids and two old farts. Those kids'll never know what hit um."

"Yeah," Sam grinned. "We just need to get a little equipment to make sure it's the old farts that come out on top."

After making boat arrangements at the marina, they got into their rental car and drove back to George Town. They stopped at a central square with a park and bought fish and chips and a cold beer from a lunch stand. Then they carried their lunch to a picnic table in a corner of the park away from other people. As soon as they were alone, Steve asked, "So what equipment are you thinking of? You have a plan?"

"First, you agree we should go in after dark when they're asleep?"

Steve took a bite of the fish and nodded.

Sam chewed a large hunk of fish, then continued, "I think our best approach is by water, but not with the boat, they might hear it, so that means wet suits and water proof pouches." He pulled out his phone and began searching the business listings in George Town. "Here, we can rent the wet suits at this place," he said pointing to the listing on the phone. "We can swim right into that boathouse and climb the stairs to check out the first and second floors. Third floor we'll have to enter from inside, which means we have to take out anyone on the first two floors and do it very quietly. You with me so far?"

"These are kids in their prime, We're . . . we're a bit past that. How you figure on taking them out quietly?"

"Tranquilizer guns."

"Tranquilizer guns? We're on our own here, Sam. We got no way to requisition such equipment. Where you going to get a tranq gun?"

"Right here, said Sam pointing at the next listing he had pulled up. "Island Veterinary Supply."

"Don't you need a license to buy that shit?"

"Probably. That's why we rent the wet suits first."

"Why will having the wet suits help us get the tranq guns?

"Because, said Sam with a big grin, we'll have a big bag."

For a moment Steve looked blank. "A big bag . . . " Then the light dawned. "You're planning on stealing them?"

"Na. Just a short term loan. Finish your lunch. We also have to hit the Private Security Supply store for plastic cuffs, earwigs, and night vision goggles."

Steve sat staring at his old friend in mild disbelief. "And here I thought you had changed in your retirement. I should have known you're still just as likely to get me in deep shit as ever."

Sam grinned for a moment, then said more seriously, "Look, Steve, you're unfortunately right, we are, shall we say past prime. And when we go in there we not only need to make sure you and me and Eddie come out unhurt, but I really don't want to kill any of those well-connected rich kids either. Not that the rotten shits don't deserve it, but I don't want to spend the rest of my retirement in a foreign prison or be constantly looking over my shoulder for those kid's papas coming after us."

Steve nodded and shoved the last bite of fish in his mouth. The two of them tossed the trash in the container and headed for the car.

"I suppose I get to carry the bag and be the thief, right?"

"Well, sure. I got the hard job."

"What job's that?"

"Talking fast enough to keep the shop keeper distracted while you stuff our *purchases* in the bag."

CHAPTER TWENTY-SIX

Whether they were Israeli guardian angels or treasure hunters, we had decided that our mysterious shadows who had followed us from the beginning of this strange trip wanted us to know they were there and had so far proven their good intentions. So, I had put the pen with their tracking and listening devices carefully back in the top of my large shoulder bag.

We finished off the sweet rolls and coffee, then Nelson said, "Breakfast is over girls. Time to get back to work and I think I may have found what we missed in Bennett's notes." He pulled up the iPad and opened to the page with Bennett's bank message.

Diana, you told me Bennett didn't make mistakes and anything he did was deliberate, but you failed to notice that in this message there is one other letter that is darker, like bank. See here?"

I looked at the line that read, "On this lovely small isle I finally found the most delightful spot of the trip. It's on a shady, protected bluff above the north **bank** and offers a spot with perfect temperature and ideal humidity."

I had to read it over twice before I saw the e in the word, the, was indeed written over. "I see. "e bank," Does that mean east bank maybe? No, it says north bank. Is there an east bank or a north bank on the island? Is it on a bluff and if so what would be there that would be atmospherically controlled to protect the paintings? Maybe we need to check out the banks again and look for . . . "

"I don't think so," said Nelson. "While I was running various searches for some clue about an e bank I accidently found a very interesting fact. Ebank is a surname here, so common, it's like Smith in the U.S. I think this clue is about a person named Ebank. As to the rest, on a bluff on the north shore etc, I don't know what it means. We just need to find someone named Ebank, who fits into Bennett's clue and was here in 1949."

"Oh, is that all," said Abbie, her voice dripping with sarcasm. "And of course that person must also be still alive. No problem."

"We won't find that set of criteria on the computer," I said. "Let's pack up and head to the public library and see if they have old phone books."

We went out to the waiting car but were disappointed to find that Mr. Johnny had to take his wife to the doctor and had sent Mr. Harry in his place. As Mr. Harry greeted us and gave us this news, he was ever bit as polite as Mr. Johnny, but there was something about his attitude that was colder, perhaps more formal than Mr. Johnny had been. I think all of us must have sensed this because we instinctively kept conversation to a minimum in the car and discussed nothing about our search.

At the George Town Public Library we met a soft spoken young black woman who introduced herself as, Miss Bertie. Like all librarians everywhere, she bent over backward to be helpful even though she was surrounded by a large group of kids who were there for the Cayman Reads program. Quietly and efficiently she made sure everyone received assistance, but in our case that assistance simply let us know that the Library had no phone directories back as far as 1949 and the only book on genealogy was a how-to book. No history of the Ebank family could be found. Like all good librarians, however, if she didn't have the information, she knew where to direct us for a further search.

By 9:00 a.m. we were standing in front of the Cayman Island National History Museum listening to a gentleman blow on the conch shell as the national flag was raised. Newly rebuilt after hurricane damage, the building looked like a two story home in a modified territorial style. It was sparking white with a red roof, looked neat as a pin and was circled by an iconic white picket fence. After the brief ceremony was over we introduced ourselves to the conch blower and complemented him on the lovely ceremony. He introduced himself as Mr. Deal. In the musical and lilting accent of the Caymanians he proudly informed us that he is the one who reintroduced the custom of blowing the conch shell and that it is now blown each morning as the flag is raised at the museum.

"What a wonderful custom," said Abbie. What was it blown for before the museum?"

"It let folks know of the arrival of a vessel. Most of us from the Caymans make our living one way or anther from the sea, so ships are very important."

While Abbie and I were chatting up Mr. Deal, Nelson was asking the girl at entrance about Mr. Ebank. He soon learned that the conch blower was one Ebank, Mr. Deal Ebank, but not the one that Miss Bertie had directed us to. The Mr. Ebank we wanted was Mr. Norman. We began to understand why these folks used their given names. Nelson was told that Mr. Norman was quite elderly and wasn't at the museum this early. With a little charm and considerable persistence, Nelson got an address where we might find Mr. Norman. He was living at a group home for the aged.

Following the custom I had noticed Mr. Johnny use, I bought a pineapple off a street vender and took it with us to the home. We were greeted warmly by the receptionist, Miss Katherine. She checked first with Mr. Norman Ebank, then returned to the desk and led us to a table on the patio where Mr. Norman was enjoying the morning sun. I gave the pineapple to Mr. Norman and thanked him for seeing us. He immediately handed it off to Miss Katherine and asked her to slice it for us. It was returned to the table in short order, sliced and served with knives, forks and small plates.

"We stopped by the museum to see you but they told us we might be able to talk with you here," I explained.

"Well," he said, here I am. What would you like to talk with me about?"

"We had spoken to Miss Bertie at the Library and . . ."

"Is that right? So you folks been to our library too? How nice. Many of our visitors just go to the snorkin' and divin' spots."

"Yes, we're not just here on vacation. We're searching for an old friend of my Uncle's. His name is Ebank and that's why Miss Bertie suggested we come and talk with you."

"Is that so? That kinda strange."

"Why would that be strange?"

"Why, because Miss Bertie's surname is Ebank too. Wonder why she send you to me."

He was still polite but a bit of suspicion had crept into his voice. "This Ebank we are looking for, if he's even still alive, would be quite elderly. She said you might know some of the older Ebanks who might have lived here a long time ago.

"Who is this Ebank man you looking for and why you lookin' for him?

"Well, it's kind of a long story," I said, "but, to keep it short. This Mr. Ebank did my uncle Bennett the favor of taking care of some things for him. Bennett always planned on getting back down here but unfortunately he died last year and in his will he left a small bequest for Mr. Ebank and asked that I try to find him and give it to him."

"He didn't leave you a given name or address or nothing?"

"Ah, you see, Bennett was here in 1949, and I don't think he remembered much more than the man's last name."

His eyes opened wider in surprise but he said nothing, waiting for more information.

"Bennett did say, however, that the man lived on a protected bluff on the north bank, what ever that means. We were hoping to find some old phone directories or Ebank family histories or something so we could try to find an Ebank who lived here in 1949."

Still, he waited me out, seeming to know I hadn't yet told everything I could. "Is there anything like that at the museum that might help us find him?"

"Hmm. A Mr. Ebank who lives on a protected bluff on the north bank, and kept something for your uncle. What exactly was he keepin' for him? Does this Mr. Ebank still have it?"

Mr. Norman was quickly zeroing in on the heart of the matter. Nothing wrong with his mind. How much did I dare tell him? Could I trust him? Oh, well, in for a penny, in for a pound.

"My uncle left four oil paintings that were very old and needed to be kept someplace they would not be damaged by humidity or heat."

Mr. Norman laughed. "So he leaves them here in the Caymans where the hurricanes come through near every year?"

I laughed too. "Yeah, that does seem a bit strange, but it's my impression that Mr. Ebank may have had an atmospherically controlled vault to keep them in."

Mr. Norman stopped laughing and jerked his head up. There was no doubt. His expression told me that all the puzzle pieces had just dropped into place and this fellow knew the answer to my question. Now it was just a matter of whether he would tell me.

He studied me for several seconds and seemed to be evaluating whether or not *he* could trust *me*. "Let me understand this story again. You got an uncle who comes here to Grand Cayman in 1949 and leaves four paintings that need special care with Mr. Ebank and never comes back for the paintings? It that right?"

I nodded, realizing I should have made up some other story, anything would have been more believable than the truth about Bennett.

"And now Mr. Bennett dies and leaves somethin' in his will for Mr. Ebank but don't leave no given name, no address or nothing."

"Yeah, I'm afraid that's about the size of it. But there is a reason that we need to find those paintings very quickly. It is vital that we find them. In fact you could say, it's a matter of life and death. Can you help us? Please!"

"What was the nature of this bequest left to Mr. Ebank?"

"My uncle said they originally agreed on $100 dollars per year. By now that would amount to sixty-three hundred. But my uncle said that with the inflation since then, I should make it ten thousand."

Mr. Norman studied my face carefully while I told him this and continued to look at me without saying anything. Nelson's amazement was fairly well hidden, but knowing him well I could see his eyes widen at this amount of bait I had just tossed out.

"And," I added, I am also offering a thousand dollar reward for anyone who can help us find him."

Finally he nodded. "Hmm, Interesting. A right hansom sum." He looked us each over for several seconds, then used both hands on the arms of his chair to push himself up. He smiled graciously and said, "Before you leave, look around our garden here. It's quite loverly."

Dismissal. My heart sank. I was sure this man could help us and I was frantic to think what else I could say to gain his confidence. I was considering telling him the whole story and throwing myself on his mercy.

Before I could think of what to say he added, "I'll make a phone call and be back in about ten minutes. Then maybe we talk some more."

CHAPTER TWENTY-SEVEN

When Mr. Norman returned he said, I think maybe this man may be able to help you and he simply handed us a slip of paper with a name, address and phone number for a fellow named Gerald Hampton Ebank, on Queens Highway. We thanked him and promised to return with his reward if this proved to the right person.

I made a quick call to the phone number we were given and received permission to drive out to meet with Mr. Gerald Ebank. The man I spoke to sounded elderly and seemed to be expecting my call.

We gave the address to Mr. Harry, and Nelson, Abbie and I sat together in the back seat with the iPad silently checking the site against Bennett's clues.

Our hopes were high as we pulled up to the security gate in front of what looked to be a Mediterranean style mansion. We announced ourselves and were greeted by a uniformed security guard who opened the gate and directed Mr. Henry to a parking spot, then escorted Nelson, Abbie and me into the house.

The entrance was absolutely breathtaking. We walked into a grand foyer with two staircases leading down into a great room. The entire wall of the great room was filled with arched windows three stories high providing a stunning ocean view. Like three country bumpkins, we stood open mouthed and fixated on the room before us.

The guard cleared his throat noisily, got our attention and said,

"If you would care to refresh yourselves before meeting with Mr. Ebank, there are powder rooms to each side of the foyer."

"Thank you," said Nelson, "that won't be necessary."

Abbie gave Nelson a look of disapproval and quietly said, "At my age, Nelson, one never passes up a powder room." Then she turned to the guard and said, "Thank you young man, I would like to use your powder room." Turning to me she added. "Diana?"

I grinned and wondered if she needed to go or just wanted to see what the foyer power room in this place would look like. "Yes, I'll join you."

Abbie took the one on the right and I took the one on the left. When we returned a few minutes later, Abbie leaned close to me and ventured a quiet, "Wow!" I smiled but said nothing. We would definitely have to share our impression of the "powder room" later.

Our guard/guide nodded and said, "If you would come this way," and led us down the stairway into the great room.

All the furniture in the great room was draped in white upholstery covers, as was the furniture in the large formal diningroom and a grand sitting room. It looked as if the place was moth-balled for the season.

We were taken into a room totally out of character with the elegant entrance. It looked as if it had once been an entertainment hall, but now seemed to be a makeshift apartment. There, our taciturn guard deposited us saying, "Mr. Ebank will be with you shortly." With that he turned and left the room, leaving us to stare around in silence.

Ten minutes passed and no one came. "Well we might as well sit down," said Nelson taking one of the chairs in a small siting area in the middle of the room.. Abbie sat on the couch.

I wondered around the room noticing the beautiful imported

hardwoods that were used on the walls and cupboards and cabinets, and was puzzled by the nasty cuts and scraps that defaced them all.

In one corner of the room was a bed and next to it an overnight stand piled with a collections of medicine bottles. Adjacent to the bed was another bathroom with no door, only a privacy curtain that was not completely closed. I looked into it and noted the safety adjustments and adaptations that had been made in there. A strong medicinal odor emanated from the room. Not exactly like the luxury of the foyer powder rooms.

On the outside wall of the room was a small alcove that jutted out onto a patio. The circular wall was all windows and glass doors giving access to both the patio and a lap pool. The door stood open allowing for a fresh cooling breeze and bird song. Inside the alcove was a small dining table and four chairs.

Across the back side of the room was a beautiful polished wooden bar that ran almost the entire length of the room. The bar was interrupted in the middle of the room, leaving an alcove that seemed to go nowhere and just stopped at a wooden wall. Then the bar started up again three feet further down and ran to the end of the room. The first section of the bar had been turned into a small but efficient kitchenette with all appliances unusually low. Here too, on the beautiful old wood of the bar, were the same cuts and scrape marks. I followed them down the long bar to the alcove and watched them go through the alcove and mysteriously stop at the wall.

In the middle of the room, between the bed and the dining area was a small siting area with a couch and two chairs and a coffee table. A large screen television could be viewed from the bed or the sitting area. All the comforts of home.

My observation and analysis made the conclusions inescapable.

Only one question remained to be answered. Was he still alive? Disturbed by that question, I finally sat down on the couch beside Abbie to await the answer.

Another ten minutes went by and a young man entered carrying a tray with tea cups, cream, sugar, lemon, spoons and napkins. He nodded shyly and smiled but said nothing. He set the tray down on the coffee table and left again, pausing briefly at the kitchenette. In five minutes the whistle on the tea kettle began to blow and we realized he must have set it to boil on the stove in the kitchenette. When he didn't return and it continued to scream, Abbie got up and went to the stove and turned off the gas fire. Though Abbie was quite short, the stove top came only to her thighs. On the counter beside the stove, she found a large pottery tea pot with tea already loaded in the infuser, so she grabbed a pot holder, picked up the tea kettle and poured the hot water into the pot. She covered the pot with a tea cosy that was laying beside it and brought the pot to our coffee table.

When the pot had time to steep and no one had returned, Abbie removed the tea cosy and said, "Well, I guess I'm Mother. Nelson, would you like some tea and how do you take it?"

He was about to answer when we heard a car tearing down the driveway. Nelson got up and walked to the windows in the dining alcove. "A black sedan pulling into the four-car garage." He reported. Then a moment later, "Someone headed our way. Maybe our host has arrived."

A young man in a business suit walked briskly up the driveway, through the patio, past the lap pool and through the door into the dining alcove. He took out his handkerchief and dotted his forehead which glistened with sweat. He blinked, trying to adjust his vision from the bright sunlight to the darkend room, surveyed the tableau and announced, "Good Afternoon. Sorry to have kept you waiting. I'm afraid I was at the office when I got the message to meet you here."

We all stared dumbly, Abbie caught mid-motion, holding the tea pot aloft above Nelson's tea cup.

He continued uncertainly. "I'm Gerald Ebank. I received a message that someone needed to talk with me urgently.

Gerald Ebank looked to be all of twenty-five years old. I could not help the incredulity and disappointment in my voice when I asked, "You're Gerald Ebank? Gerald Hampton Ebank?"

The tone of his answer let me know he was somewhat affronted by my question. "Yes, and just who did you say you were?"

"I'm, . . . I'm sorry, Mr. Ebank. I'm Diana Hunter and it's just that I was looking for someone older by the name of Gerald Ebank, Perhaps your father has the same name?"

"No, I'm afraid not."

I wasn't sure what to say from there. Abbie filled in. "Mr. Ebank, would you care for a cup tea?"

"Ah, yes, thank you. It looks like my staff has left you somewhat on your own. Sorry. We don't get many guests here these days and the small staff that's still here is not experienced in dealing with guests." He took the other chair and I introduced Nelson as my attorney and Abbie as my Aunt. Abbie poured tea all around.

"Well," said Mr. Ebank," if I am not what you were expecting, may I ask who is the person you are looking for and why are you seeking him?"

"I believe my great uncle, Bennett Hunter, had a friend by that name and he lived here in Grand Cayman. When I found that name I was certain it had to be the right person. Do you by chance have a grandfather or an uncle who has the same name. It's really very important, in fact it is truly a matter of life and death that I find my uncle's friend."

"My, a matter of life and death," he said mockingly. "That sounds rather dramatic. Perhaps you could tell me more about the matter."

"Yes, I guess it does sound rather melodramatic, but it is unfortunately true and unless you can help us someone will die. When I called before I spoke to someone with an older sounding voice and that person seemed to know the name Bennett Hunter. Could I please speak to that person?"

"I'm sorry, but I'm afraid there is no one else living here but me, and a skeleton staff, of course."

I only had a few moments after Mr. Ebank arrived, but before he had got there, I'd had a good half an hour to observe, collect and analyze data. The idea that this healthy young man was the person living in this house was ludicrous. If I had more time, or if the circumstances were less dire, I might have been more courteous and less direct, but I had played all the games I was going to play.

"I'm sorry, Mr. Ebank, or who ever you really are, but I'm quite certain that is not true."

"What!" He looked stunned and glanced around the room as if someone or something would come to his rescue. The only person in the room, other than us, was the shy young man who had brought in the tea tray and had now returned with cakes.

"You are not the person who lives here. That is a lie, and I don't have time to suffer fools. The person who lives in this room is confined to a wheel chair. The lovely wood of the bar and the walls is all slashed at the same height all around the room, cut and scraped by the chair. All the cupboards and cabinets more than about four and a half feet off the floor are empty. All dishes, pots, pans, wines, liquor bottles etc are on the lower shelves. The door has been removed from the bathroom and replaced by a curtain for easy accesses of the wheel chair. The bathroom has been retrofitted with safety bars for an elderly person."

I walked over to the alcove in the center of the bar. "There is an alcove here that seems to lead nowhere, yet scratch marks from the chair go through here as if this is actually a door to another room."

As I said that I reached up and pushed on a well worn spot in the wood and the wood panel began to open. As it started to open Mr. Ebank jumped from his chair and ran toward me saying, "Stop, you have no right, you can't go in there."

As the door opened I saw a small man sitting in a wheel chair, grey hair, narrow shoulders, blue eyes behind coke bottle lenses. He smiled revealing near perfect teeth."

I looked at him and said, "The real Mr. Ebank, I presume?"

He raised his hands, elbows resting on the chair arms and began to applaud. "Well done, my dear. I didn't know Bennett had a niece, but certainly if he did, she would be just like you. That is to say, she would be just like him."

"Grandpa, don't jump to conclusions, You can't know . . ." Turning to the young man who brought in the tea cakes, he said, "Sandy, call the guards. Put these people off the property."

CHAPTER TWENTY-EIGHT

"Jerry, please be still. These people are my guests though they have had little proper hospitality so far. Diana, Please pardon my grandson. He acts only out of concern for my welfare. When he heard a stranger was coming to the house he insisted on meeting you first."

"Well, I guess I would want to protect my grandfather too, if I had one."

"I appreciate your understanding," he said as he moved his wheel chair toward the main room, obviously expecting me to step aside as he wheeled himself over to the coffee table.

Abbie, please, could you pour me a bit of tea with a little milk and sugar?"

He knew our names, so he had evidently been listening and probably watching us.

"I guess at this point there is no need for introductions," I said, "but I must ask, are you the Mr. Ebank who knew my uncle Bennett?"

"Yes. And when I heard you were here I tried to contact Bennett Hunter's private secretary to verify that he had in deed passed on and to verity your relationship; but so far I have not heard back from him."

I felt a slight panic at the news that Robert James was unreachable. Then I considered the day and the time. Looking at my watch I said, "Today's his marketing day. He will be in town all morning, usually home about noon unless he lunches in town. I believe you're in the same time zone here so you should be hearing from him within an hour."

"Wonderful, then perhaps we might have a bite of lunch together and get acquainted. Then we can discuss the paintings after lunch."

"The paintings? Then you know why I'm here?"

He laughed. "Of course I know why you're here. I should imagine everyone on the island would know by now."

Taken aback, I looked around to Abbie and Nelson and saw they too registered alarm at this statement. "Why and how would everyone on the island know why I'm here?"

"It's a small island, my dear, and you've talked about it all over town."

"I have not. I have spoken to five banks, one librarian, and one museum docent and the only one I told about the paintings was the docent who gave me your name and address not two hours ago."

He sipped his tea and waved his hand to wave off my denial. "Miss Hunter, you could have stopped with telling one bank and everyone would know."

"But, I thought the Cayman's had such great bank secrecy laws."

"Oh, we do if you pay us to keep a bank account for you. But if a stranger walks in, asking about museum vaults and inherited accounts, that sounds very much like there is a hidden treasure story. That means you aren't an account holder, you're gossip. And lost treasure is the kind of gossip we islanders love best. Add to that the fact that everyone knows I moved the vault that was in my bank to my home in order to store same mysterious paintings . . . well."

The enormity of this disaster was overwhelming.

"You look a bit pale, Diana. Perhaps you better sit down. Why is this a problem?"

"I'm afraid, Mr. Ebank, I have inadvertently placed you in great danger."

His grandson said, "I knew there would be trouble from this. What kind of danger?"

"I'm sure it is nothing we can't handle," said the old man, but perhaps you had better tell us why you seek the paintings and what sort of danger they represent. But let's not do it on an empty stomach. Jerry, I had Mira prepare a bit of lunch. Would you please tell her we're ready for it."

Mr. Ebank wheeled himself over to the wine rack, selected a bottle and wheeled back to Nelson. "Young man would you be kind enough to cork that and get five glasses?

"Yes sir, and the cork screw is where?"

"Over there on that hook at the end of the bar. Come Ladies, let's move to the dinning table. If we're lucky you can see some of the creatures who come to drink from my pool. Now tell me, Diana, who is after the pictures and what sort of danger do they pose?"

I saw no point in mincing words and decided to tell the tale as briefly as possible but not hold back any pertinent data. "Do you know how Bennett originally came by those paintings?"

"Not exactly. I do know, however, they were originally stolen by the Nazis. You don't have Nazis after you at this late date I trust."

"No. After the war ended, the paintings were in a large stash of Nazi loot found and being guarded by the U.S. Army. The officer in charge took several pieces for himself and had them shipped home to Texas. Bennett found out about it but when he tried to report the officer he quickly learned that the guy was too well connected. If Bennett made formal accusations, he would be the one who ended up in the brig. So he kept quiet but he and a friend decided to steal the art back and try to find the rightful owners. They raided they officer's home and got away with the art, but were being closely pursued. Fleeing to the West coast they signed on with the first freighter that would take them and sailed out of Los Angeles harbor with the art in a trunk."

"Ah, and that's how he ended up here with the art. That answers a few questions I've had for many years. At the time, the bank I owned had one of the few museum quality vaults this side of New York. He left the paintings with me and promised to return and collect them, but so far all he as done is continue the rental payment. When I sold the bank and retired I had to move the vault to my home because the new owner felt it was an unnecessary expense to the bank. So why are these paintings suddenly a matter of life and death?"

About five weeks ago my father was kidnaped in Turkey by four young men, one of whom is the grandson of the fellow who stole the art from the Army stockpile. His family has been hunting for that art and nursing the grudge against Bennett for three generation. This grandson, Marty Adacci, found some notes that Bennett left behind, God know where, but the notes were from the voyage when he sailed from Los Angeles to New York."

At the mention of the grandson's name Ebank drew in a sharp breath that hissed through his teeth. His face then froze into an attempt at a poker face. Like many who try to hide an emotional reaction however, Ebank's blank look made his response more obvious. The name was obviously known to him and was unnerving.

I continued, watching him closely now for further reaction. "The notes left tantalizing clues as to where he had stashed the art but were in a sort of make-shift code. Marty and his college friends first tried to find the art themselves and couldn't. Then he grabbed my father and tried to beat him into telling where the art was hidden. Dad didn't know anything about the art and couldn't decipher the codes left in Bennett's notes. Then they decided that since I was Bennett's heir, I would be able to find the art for them. They're holding my father and say they'll kill him if I don't find and return their art.

Ebank studied his hands for a few moments then my face. Finally he formed a question. "And if you ransom your father with this art, do you believe they will release him alive?"

I hesitated a moment wondering how the truth would affect him, but since he was now also in danger, I had to tell him. Besides the way he had phrased his question made me believe he already had his own answer.

"No. In fact we believe that once they have the art, they intend to kill us all. Now that my search has implicated you, it's possible they might be a threat to you as well."

His voice filled with anger and he asked, "And just what is it you have learned that makes you believe these are the sort of young men who go around murdering people?"

"They're college students who belong to a senior society that is linked to organized crime. Supposedly, they can't be full members until they've killed someone.

He nodded. "The Acclivitous Society." It was a statement, not a question and he seemed to know exactly what it meant. He looked up at me with fear on his face and asked, "Is one of the Banks you spoke to the Medallion Bank of Italy?"

"Yes, why?"

His cook had arrived with a tray of lovely smelling food. He said to her sharply, "Take it away, Mira."

Startled, she asked, "Is there something wrong with the lunch sir?"

He answered her, "Our guests won't have time for lunch."

He stared at me a moment then said, "It's really too bad your research wasn't a bit more thorough, Miss Hunter. The President and two board officers of the Medallion are alumni of the Acclivitous Society."

He let the weight of that information sink in then asked, "Where and how do you intend to make the exchange for your father?"

"We haven't quite worked that out yet. Why?"

"Jerry, please take Diana and her friends to the vault. Wrap the pictures well for travel and help put them into her car, quickly."

He turned to me. Biting off his words with anger he said, "My advice would be that you do not try the exchange on the island. It is a small island with strong family relationships. In face of those relationships, it could be a mistake to trust the local officials or the police. You would be better off to get back to U.S. soil as soon as possible." Then without another word, he rolled the wheel chair to the alcove, scraping the sides of the bar as he went, pushed open the panel at the back of the alcove and disappeared into the next room.

CHAPTER TWENTY-NINE

It was about five in the afternoon. Sam and Steve were just getting settled into their surveillance spot at the public dock. They had food for supper and figured they would be here for several hours until the lights went out and the kidnapers went to sleep. They were closer to the house than before, and had a good view of the right side of the house, but could barely see the left side with the boathouse. The wet suits were left in the bag until time to suit up and go into the house, but they had opened the tranquilizer guns and loaded a dart each to make sure they were in working order. They then loaded the guns and extra darts into the waterproof pouches that could be belted around their waists.

Steve was on watch while Sam typed a text message to Diana letting her know their progress on finding her father. He didn't write details on the planned rescue, but wanted her to know they hoped to have Eddie safely out of the kidnapper's hands that night. He had neither finished nor sent the message before everything changed.

Loud yelling erupted from the house. A door slammed and two of the gang stomped out and headed for the garage. The third yelled something and was answered by the other two.

Sam closed his phone and dropped it into his pants pocket. He picked up the binoculars and could see the two going to the garage

were Marty Adacci and Rick Myers. The one at the door was Frank
Caminari. Frank yelled again and this time accompanied his words with
a warning gun shot into the garage wall. That brought Marty and Rick
up short. More discussion followed. Sam and Steve could hear voices
but not make out the words. Then Rick went into the house with Frank.
When they reappeared, all three went into the garage, the door went up
and the car pulled out and headed at high speed down Boggy Sand
Road toward George Town.

Sam and Steve required no discussion. The kidnapers had left
without Eddie. Sam feared that could mean only one thing. "God damn,
son of a bitch," he cussed under his breath as he started the engine on
the cabin cruiser. He ran at high speed toward the boathouse. No time
for stealth now. They would probably find Eddie dead, but as Sam ran
the boat up to the boathouse he had to pray his friend might still be
alive, that he might somehow still save the terrible foul up. Once again
he had been sitting on his ass in surveillance when he should have just
entered guns blazing before it was too late.

CHAPTER THIRTY

The four oil paintings hanging on the wall in the vault were quickly taken down, cushioned with foam and wrapped in paper, then boxed. All supplies used were from boxes marked *archival quality* so I could at least hope Jerry and the two staff members knew what they were doing.

I had only a few moments to look at the paintings as Jerry wrapped them. There were two portraits, one Madonna and child, and the fourth was a still life. I didn't recognize the works and didn't have time to search for signatures, but they matched the photos sent on the iPad.

As Jerry and his staff carried the paintings to our car I walked over out of ear shot and called Sam on my secure phone. I got his voice mail and left a message. "Sam, we have the paintings and are heading back to the motel, however, we are fully blown. News of our arrival and purpose is all over the island and one of the banks I talked to is evidently run by Acclivitous Society members. We'll gather our stuff and head to the plane and leave all there with the pilots for safe-keeping. Please meet us at the plane to work out problems on the exchange."

In less than twenty minutes from the time Mr. Ebank gave the order, the paintings were all stowed in the trunk of our car and we were given the bum's rush off the property. I was sure the gentleman at the group home who gave us his name also told Mr Ebank about the ten thousand dollar bequest but Ebank didn't even ask about it. He just wanted us gone. Considering the people we were dealing with, I couldn't really blame him. He looked to have enough wealth that the bequest would not be his top priority under the circumstances.

Our driver had shown some interest in our boxes but was too busy on his cell phone to pay too much attention. That should have alerted me, but I was too busy with other problems.

We rode quietly back to the motel, not wanting to talk in front of the driver and at a loss as to what to say anyway. When we got back the driver pulled up in front of the motel room, opened the trunk, but made no effort to help us unload the boxes. Abbie and I each took one, Nelson grabbed the other two, and I dug for my key to the motel door.

When the door swung open and I saw lights on, I immediately stopped and started to turn around. Two guns clicked as their owners drew back the hammer on their revolvers. I was half turned toward the parking lot and saw that one of those guns was being held by our driver, Mr. Harry. I turned back to the room and saw three young men, one of them armed, pointing his gun at us.

"You don't need the guns. I told you, I'd trade the art for my dad," I was relatively calm until I looked around the room and realized all three of these guys were here and my father was no where in sight. I looked each of them in the face, trying to read what was hidden there. Trying to keep my voice calm and not quite succeeding, I asked, "I've kept my end of the bargain, where is my father?"

Marty, who was not armed, but was covered by both the driver and Frank Caminari, walked over to me. Without warning he swung his fist at my face as he shouted, "Here's my part of the bargain bitch." I ducked his punch and held up the art box. His fist hit the corner of the box and he yelled and cursed. As he raised his arm for a second shot, Nelson stepped between us and landed a one-two punch to Marty's face and gut that put him on the floor. Frank aimed his gun at Nelson, but fired after Nelson had jumped on Marty on the floor. He hit the mirror over the bed and shattered it.

Marty yelled, Jesus, Frankie, don't shoot! You'll have the cops here."

Abbie stepped behind Frank, did a whirling kick that caught Frank behind the knees, flipping him backwards. As he landed on his back on the floor, he accidently fired again, this time narrowly missing Rick Myers who had joined in the fight between Nelson and Marty.

Abbie landed a second kick on the Frank's hand and knocked the gun to the floor. Picking up the gun she aimed it at Frank saying, "Stay right where you are, kid, unless you want to lose your family jewels."

The driver stood at the door, gun aiming variously at several moving targets. When Marty yelled again, "I said don't shoot, you fucking idiot." The driver, not sure what to do, lowered his pistol.

Still holding onto the picture I'd carried in, I swung the box and connected with the driver's wrists. He let out a cry and dropped the gun, which I retrieved and motioned Mr. Harry over to where Frank lay on the floor.

Marty Adacci and Rick Myers were no match for Nelson. I had seen him take out two truly deadly opponents in the past and didn't try to interrupt as Nelson beat the stuffing out of the two boys. When all were quietly subdued, I walked over to Marty and said in deadly seriousness, "I'll only give you one chance to answer me before I start putting bullets in your body. "Where is my father?"

CHAPTER THIRTY-ONE

Sam and Steve pulled their cabin cruiser up to the wall around the house and nosed it in as close as they could to the speedboat in the boat house. They strapped on the only weapons they had, the tranquilizer guns, and started for the house. They had to step onto the speedboat and walk on the hull to where they could reach the steps. Steve made it. Sam slipped and fell into the water. Soaked to the arm pits, he grabbed hold of the bottom rail of the ladder and pulled himself up the steps and onto the first floor deck.

Trying the side door they found it locked. Rather than taking the time to break in, they ran around to the garage side of the house where they knew the gang had left the door, not only unlocked, but standing open. They pulled the tranquilizer guns and entered the darkened house through the kitchen. From the second floor they heard voices but quickly concluded by the laugh track that it was a television that had been left on. They carefully checked the first floor. Finding no one, they started up the stairs. The only sound they made was the soft wet squish of Sam's soaked shoes and pants. One by one they checked the bedrooms, working their way to the one that had the television playing. The light was on and they could see a lump under the sheet and see Eddie's grey head lying on the pillow. Sam looked around the room, but saw no one else and walked over to the bed. He reached down to check Eddies neck for a pulse. Just as he touched him Eddie jumped, turned over to face him and shouted, "What the hell . . ."

Sam also jumped and squeezed the trigger on the tranquilizer gun. With a loud pop it planted a dart in the bed. Sam yelled joyfully, "Eddie, you're alive!"

All three stared at the dart. "So far," answered Eddie, then asked, "Sam, how the hell . . . What are you doing here?"

"Rescuing you from your kidnappers. How come they left you alone?"

"They got a call saying Diana had the art work. Marty told Caminari kid to stay here and off me as soon as they called to say they really had the art. Frankie didn't trust Marty and insisted they all go for the art and all do me at the same time."

"So are they all are headed for Diana?"

"Yeah, I think the plan is to kill Diana and Abbie as soon as they have the art. We got to get to her. Can you get me out of this thing?" He held up his left wrist that was attached by a pair of handcuffs to a chain that was attached by another set of cuffs to the bedstead.

While Steve picked the lock on the cuffs, Sam pulled out his phone to call Diana. The phone had been in his pants pocket and was soaked and dead. He walked over to the phone on the dresser but Eddie said, "Don't even bother. The phones to the house were turned off for the season. They all use cell phones."

"Steve, do you have your cell phone?" asked Sam.

He felt his pockets and answered, "I think I left it on the boat." He opened the cuff and removed it from Eddie's wrist. "Let's get the hell out of here."

When Eddie stood, both Steve and Sam stared. "You got any

clothes?" ask Steve.

"Oh," said Eddie, as if just noticing his nudity. "Thanks to my darling daughter, I've gotten quite used to living *au naturel*. I think there's a very dirty pair of jeans and a t-shirt in the closet."

"You get dressed and I'll go to the boat and call Diana with Steve's cell."

As Eddie was pulling the t-shirt on over his jeans, he and Steve heard a yell from Sam out by the boathouse. He cursed at top volume "God damn, son of a bitch!" Steve ran for the boathouse, Eddie followed as soon as he could get his shoes on.

They found Sam standing on the front deck of the house, hands on his hips, looking out to sea. There, five hundred yards or more off shore, floated the cabin cruiser.

Without a word, Eddie turned, went into house and a couple minutes later came back and handed Sam a set of keys. With a grin and a smart-ass tone in his voice he said, "This one is to the speed boat. Remember to tie it up when we get to the dock."

They all got into the speed boat and headed for the public dock where they had left their car. As they climbed into the car, Sam said, "The last message I had from Diana said they had the paintings and were going to their motel to get their stuff. Then they were going to the plane to stash the art and wait for us to make plans for the exchange. She won't have any idea the gang is coming after her. We'll head for the motel first and hope to hell we get to her in time."

CHAPTER THIRTY-TWO

Marty hesitated before answering my question. I was too angry and too worried for any delays. I drew back the gun and slammed it as hard as I could into Marty's face. "Where's my dad?" I repeated.

Marty howled with pain and waved me off with both hands. Blood gushing from his broken lip he said, "He's at the house."

"What house? Where?"

"He's at Frankie Caminari's house, just up the coast about nine kilometers away."

I checked the cylinder on the old .45 caliber revolver I had taken away from Mr. Harry. All six chambers were loaded. With deadly intent, I pulled back the hammer, pointed the pistol directly between Marty's eyes and asked, "Is he alive or dead?"

Marty put up both hands as if he could stop the bullet from hitting his head. "He's alive, he's fine, he even has a tan and has gained weight. I swear to God. Please don't shoot. He's alive."

I hesitated several seconds as I stared at Marty's face trying to read, lie or truth.

"Nelson, please tie Mr. Harry, gag him and secure him to the bed. Then tie Rick, Frankie, and Marty with their hands behind their backs. Toss Marty and Rick into the trunk of the car. If any of them try to resist, Abbie and I will shoot." I looked at the three students now seated on the floor. "If we get out to Frankie's house and my father is either not there or is dead, you all die. Is all that clear fellas?"

They all answered quickly in the affirmative, all assuring me my father was alive.

Abbie and Nelson both looked at me and I knew they were wondering if I meant it, but of course, said nothing. At that moment, I thought I meant it and believed I could do it.

Once they were all secured, we loaded the paintings in the front passenger seat of car. The rest of our belongings could wait, but I couldn't leave the paintings in the motel. Jo Jo was again nestled in the bottom of my large shoulder bag along with my plastic gun, but they were now wrapped in a hand towels rather than my underwear.

"Nelson, please drive. Abbie and I'll sit in the back seat with Frankie while he gives you directions to his house." I looked down at Rick and Marty in the large car trunk. With malice I added, "If you find any potholes in the road on the way, hit them hard," then slammed the trunk closed. The use of such petty power only showed how truly helpless I felt.

It only took about twelve minutes to get to the house. We unloaded all our passengers and marched them into the house. Marty led us upstairs to a bedroom where the TV was still playing, but the room was empty. "Where is he?" I yelled?

"I don't know," answered Marty panic stricken. "He must have escaped. Honest to God, we left him here safe. Rick, Frankie, did you check that hand cuff? Damn it Frankie, I told you one of us should stay here with him. No, you had to insist on going along. Look, Diana, there's the handcuffs and the chain. See, we even left the chain long enough so he could move around the room, go to the bathroom."

As Marty prattled on, literally arguing for his life, I surveyed the room looking for some sign that would tell me if my father was alive or dead.

Abbie searched the bathroom and closet. "What was he wearing when you left him?, asked Abbie.

Frankie looked embarrassed and with a side-long glance at me answered, "Nothing."

Abbie asked, "Did he have clothes to wear?"

"Sure answered Frankie, in the closet there."

Abbie pulled open the closet door to show us that the closet was empty.

Nelson pointed to a dart sticking into the covers. He reached down, pulled the dart out, read the writing on the side and smelled it. He turned to Marty. "Did you boys shoot him with a tranquilizer?"

Marty stared dumb-founded at the needle. "Jesus, no. Frankie, did you do this when you came back in to tie him up?"

"No, no. We don't even have any of that shit. I never saw that before. I swear."

Abbie examined the bed and said, "Looks like that dart was shot into the bed. See the spot here?"

I picked up the handcuff and chain and noted the scratch marks around the keyhole. Someone had picked the lock. Not hard to do on these old style hand cuffs. I examined the rumpled bed, the empty closet, and then found myself staring distractedly at the floor. There was a large wet spot on the floor near the bed and smaller spots, foot prints, going both direction, into the room and back out of it again. I had stopped even listening to Marty's frantic explanations. Handing the gun I held to Nelson, I turned and followed the wet foot prints out of the room.

Marty's high frightened voice trailed off. I looked over my

shoulder and realized Nelson was herding the rest of them to follow me. The wet prints led us down the stairs and out to the front deck and around to the boathouse. I looked into the empty boathouse and asked, "Frankie do you own a boat?"

Still over by the front of the house, Frankie said, "Well, yeah, it's right there in the . . . " Then he looked over at the empty boat house. "Holy shit! He not only got away, he stole our boat."

I looked at the three kidnappers who didn't look or sound so tough at this point. Then I looked out to the center of the bay and saw a cabin cruiser that seemed to be floating freely in the middle of the outbound lane. "Frankie, is that your boat floating out there in the middle of the bay?"

"That cabin cruiser. Hell no. I got a speedboat."

I turned to Abbie and asked, "Please hand me that revolver you took away from Frankie. All three boys began to beg for their lives, swearing they had left my dad alive.

I yelled, "Shut up! All of you be quiet."

Even Nelson put in his two cents. "Diana, self-defense is one thing, but not this . . ."

I gave him a disgusted look and under my breath said,. "Oh, Nelson, for crying out loud! What do you think of me?"

I turned to the boys. "Frankie, where in the house do you keep this gun?

He answered, "Honest, we didn't kill . . . "

"Frankie, just answer the damn question. Where in your house do you stow this gun.

Confused, but obedient, he answered,"In the bottom right-hand drawer of the desk in the den."

"Thank you," I said. "Nelson, please load our little school boys back into the car. This time they can all three go into the trunk," I walked into the house. Inside I wiped down the gun, placed it in the desk drawer, then returned to the front deck.

As we climbed back into the car, Nelson asked, "Where to now?"

"I'm not sure yet whether it will be the motel or the airport, but I suspect we will get a call anytime now letting me know. No sooner had I said that than my secure phone rang. Caller ID showed the name of our motel. I answered, but before I could say anything more than "Hello," Sam was practically yelling in my ear, "Diana, don't kill those kids. Your dad's alive. He's fine and right here with me. Don't kill the kids."

"Whoa, ease off Sam, I figured that out."

"You did?"

"Just one thing I don't know yet."

"What?"

"Which one of you two fell in the water?"

"Ah, . . . that would be me."

I chuckled. "Please don't tell me it was also you, the great mariner of San Pedro, who forgot to tie off your boat?"

"You know, Diana, you can be a real smart-ass at the worst possible times."

I laughed. "I assume you've been talking to Mr. Harry. Is he still tied up there in the motel room?"

"So far, why?"

"Better leave him there until we can get ourselves and the artwork onto the plane and headed for the states. These damn kids have a lot of powerful contacts here."

"You have the boys with you?"

"Yes, see you at the airport."

We headed into town and made a quick stop at the motel to pick up our bags. While there, I unloaded and wiped down Mr. Harry's pistol and his bullets. I showed him where I was stowing the bullets in the top dresser drawer and then returned the empty pistol to his shoulder holster. As he glared at me I said, "Don't worry, Mr. Harry. It's clean and unfired. There'll be someone along to untie you soon."

I wrote out a check to Mr. Norman Ebank for $1000.00 and a second check to the museum restoration fund for $10,000. On the motel's note paper, I wrote a short thank-you to Mr. Norman for helping us find the right Mr. Ebank. I explained that it turned out that my uncle had been paying for storage of the art all those years, so I had decided to donate the ten thousand to the museum instead. I put all three items in an envelope with the motel return address, addressed it to Norman Ebank at the retirement home, and sealed it. I would drop it in the first mail box we found.

I had called ahead to our pilots and they told me my plane was fueled and that we could be cleared for take off as soon as we could get aboard.

We pulled up to the gate at the Cayman Corporate Jet Air terminal and announced ourselves over the speaker. The gate opened and we drove in and parked in front of the office reception area. One of the great advantages of private jets is that around the world they are serviced by private terminals built on the same airport campus, but off by themselves with their own entrance, security, and personnel. There is no need to slog your way through crowds of passengers and be inspected by airport security. The corporations that fly such jets provide all necessary information to the terminals ahead of time so clearance is pretty well done by the time you arrive at the airport. Of course, passengers must still fill out and turn in all necessary customs declarations, but it becomes a simple formality.

Nelson grabbed a luggage cart and we loaded it with our three suitcases, four boxes with paintings and miscellaneous bags.

Abbie asked, "What are we going to do with the boys?"

"Leave the little bastards in the trunk. Once we're in the air, we'll call back and have someone let them out."

We turned to enter the terminal and saw three armed security guards charging down on us, guns drawn. They had been waiting in a black SUV with darkened windows that had been parked just a few spaces down the lot.

One of them said, "Diana Hunter, stop right there. You're under arrest for kidnaping and art theft." The badges on the shoulders of their uniforms read, Medallion Bank Security. Not the police, so the boys had somehow contacted a member of their Acclivitous Society at the bank.

The guard walked up to Nelson, held out his hand and demanded, "Give me the keys to the car."

"They're in the ignition. Help yourself."

The guard walked over to the car, reached in for the keys, and pulled the latch that opened the trunk. He knew exactly where the boys were. As Rick, Marty and Frankie stepped out of the trunk their hands were free and Marty was displaying a pocket knife and a cell phone. He swaggered over to me, an evil grin replacing the whimpering frightened look he displayed before. "Pretty dumb not to frisk us, right bitch?"

"You want us to take them into the police station Mr. Adacci?"

"Oh, no," he answered, his voice filled with wrath, "She was kind enough to give us a ride." Marty looked at me with pure hatred. "Now we're going to do the same for her, and her friends. We've got a private jet, Diana. We'll give you a ride back to the states, half way back anyway." He laughed. "We'll be happy to drop you off somewhere along the way, like mid-ocean."

I had also threatened to kill him and his friends so this was no more than I had said, yet I knew now that mine had been just anger lashing out. I could never have killed them in cold blood. As Nelson had said, that was different than self-defense. But I knew that for Marty, it wasn't idle talk. Murder was part of his real world, the initiation into his club, the attainment of man-hood. If they got us onto their plane, they would shove us out at thirty thousand feet and laugh as they did it.

He turned back to the guards. "Take them into the terminal. As soon as they pull up our plane you can help them aboard and tie them up. Don't worry about the guy at the desk. He'll do as he's told and look the other way."

Marty turned back to me. "No seat belts though. No pot holes in the sky, but I'm sure our pilots can find a bit of turbulence to bounce you around a bit."

Marty nodded and his wing men opened the reflective glass doors that obscured the terminal office from outside view. We all entered, first Abbie, Nelson and I with the luggage cart, followed by the three guards, then Marty and last, Frankie and Rick.

A few feet inside the door, Sam jumped and disarmed the guard on the left, James the one on the right, and Dad took out the one in the middle. Marty, Rick and Frankie, started to join the fray but saw who was now holding the guns and pulled up short. Marty took a quick look around, eyed the door, then turned to make a run for it. Nelson laid him out on the floor with one blow, and the other two just stood there too surprised and dazed to make a move.

Marty stood up carefully and joined his two buddies. All three stared in amazement at Dad, then turned and looked at Sam and Steve. "Who the hell are you guys?

Sam pulled out a badge and said. "FBI. And you boys will be facing charges of kidnaping."

"Oh, no they won't," said one of the guards. "You have no jurisdiction here."

Sam looked at his shoulder patch and said, "Just what sort of jurisdiction do Bank dicks have in this matter?"

Before the guard could answer, two men in Police uniforms walked into the lobby from an inner door. With them was the lone front desk security employee for Cayman Corporate Jet Terminal. They crossed the lobby and stopped in front of Sam.

The men in police uniforms were both short, had long lean faces, olive complexions, and looked almost like they could be brothers. When they spoke their accent was not the lilting island one we had come to know. It sounded rather like a Middle Eastern accent.

Abbie and Nelson both looked from the policemen to me, recognition in their eyes, their lips ready to form a question. I tried to hide a grin and gave them a slight negative shake of my head.

The first one addressed Sam. "They have no jurisdiction, of course, and these guards as well as the security company that employs them will answer to the Royal Island Police Service which now has jurisdiction over all private security firms."

The two policemen then turned to the bank guards. "What are you men doing at the airport? Why are you drawing weapons on visitors to our country?" He pulled out a notebook "I'll need all your names and badge numbers."

 As the first officer took down the names, the second one turned to Sam. "We will also need their weapons." Sam, Steve and Dad all reluctantly turned over the guns.

I watched as a jet pulled up in front of the terminal. The door opened and the boarding steps were lowered. Marty, Frankie and Rick were all turned toward us and watched silently to see what was going to happen next. Abbie stood next to me and leaned in close to whisper, "Aren't those the . . ." I cut her off with a warning look.

After taking their names, confiscating their weapons, and giving them a thorough dressing down, the police allowed the guards to leave the terminal, but instructed them to report to police headquarters the following morning. Then the officers turned to Sam. "Now, gentleman, as to the question of jurisdiction, you would have none either, even if you really were FBI, Mr. Sam Dehany."

Sam didn't miss a beat. "Officer, those three young men kidnaped our friend here and have held him prisoner for over four weeks. We would like to have them arrested and we are ready to file a complaint."

Marty yelled, "That's a lie. We're not kidnappers. We're just college students. See this, he said pointing to the bruises and cuts on his face. That bitch over there did this to me."

The officer examined his face. "Hmm, you let a little woman do that to you?"

Changing the subject, Marty charged. "They stole art work that belongs to our family. I was just trying to get it back."

"Hmm, yes. I have a rather lengthy report on this art work from a banker. I assume the owner was planning to report this art and it's value on the proper customs form. Yes? Where is the art?"

"It's right over there on their luggage cart," said Marty.

"I'll need to examine it," said the officer. He turned to Nelson.

"Please open the boxes and unwrap it."

Nelson gave me a questioning look. I replied with a very slight nod of my head. Reluctantly, Nelson opened the boxes. After examining the paintings the officer turned to Marty. "You claim this art was in your family's possession?"

"Yes, I can prove it." He dug out his wallet and pulled out an old black and white photo. "See here. That's my granddad and all those pictures. That's our home in Texas."

"Yes, I see. With a smile and an unidentifiable tone in his voice he added, "Perhaps that does confirm it. I will need that photograph for evidence," he said taking the photo. "Our orders are to see that you and your art are loaded onto that plane. There is only one little problem."

He walked over to me. "There is a small statuette that seems to be missing. I'm sorry, Ms. Hunter, but I will need to search your purse."

I hesitated a moment, then handed it over to him. He removed my personal items and laid them on the tray of the luggage cart. Then he hauled out Jo Jo, opened the towel, and gazed admiringly at the gleaming little statuette. Then he smiled, reached down and picked up the pen from among the things on the tray. He opened it briefly to make sure it was the right one, then said, "Might I borrow your pen, Ms. Hunter?"

I smiled back. "Help yourself. Don't think I'll be needing it anymore."

He leaned close and whispered, "Our sympathies for the loss of your uncle. He was a good man. We worked with him many times."

Boxing up the paintings again, the officer said, Here boys, you carry the art and we will see you safely aboard your plane.

The five of them filed out the door, across the tarmac, and

climbed up the stairs, paintings, Jo Jo and all.

The six of us stood silently watching as the stairs were retracted and the door closed and locked down. Then Steve said, "Hey, the cops never got off and came back."

I could hold it no longer and burst out in laughter. Abbie, who was now in Dad's arms, also started laughing and Nelson joined. Sam, Steve and Dad stared at us like we were nuts.

"What's so damn funny," asked Sam. Those little bastards just walked off with all the art."

"The plane," I said through my laughter. "Look at the logo on the plane."

As the plane backed out and began its turn toward the runway, the logo was clearly visible.

"El Al?" Steve looked baffled. "Why are they flying out of here on El Al?"

Sam asked, "Were those the two guy who were following you girls around?"

Abbie, Nelson and I all answered, "Yes!"

"So they were Israeli."

Still not quite in on the joke, Steve asked, "So why did the Israelis take the boys as well as the art?"

"Well," I answered, "if it was in the states the charge would probably be possession of stolen property. Since it's Israel and the art was looted by the Nazis, I'm not sure exactly what they'll call it, but I suspect our game loving college boys will have several unpleasant years to consider the history and true ownership of that art."

The officer from the Cayman Corporate Jet Terminal was back at his desk, looking as if nothing at all unusual had taken place in his terminal. He smiled up at us and said, "Ladies and Gentlemen, I believe that is your plane pulling up. Would you please step to the desk for your check-in and customs procedures.

I looked out on the tarmac and checked the plane to make sure it really was my plane and not the one belonging to the kidnapers.

Sam and Steve looked on approvingly as Dad and Abbie were locked in each others arms and lost in a long kiss. Nelson took that as a cue and walked over and put his arms around me and kissed me gently.

My phone rang and I got a brief message from our plane crew, Bob, Sparks and Danny.

"Well gang, our plane crew says there's cold drinks and hot food aboard. Let's head home?"

Nelson shook his head and held me tightly in his arms. "We have lovely penthouse stateroom waiting aboard the *Roaming Dreamer*. Let them rush home on the jet. You and I have to finish a discussion about Baja.

Michael and Joan Francis on a cruise

Joan Francis is a licensed private investigator and owner of Francis Pacific Investigations. She has also worked as a librarian and a newspaper reporter and says each of these jobs is just a different method for doing the same task: providing information.

She spent her childhood in small mining towns and camps in the western United States and in South America with her two sisters, mother, and mining engineer father. Moving from place to place as her father opened up new mine sites, she attended fifteen schools before graduating with a B.A. in history from the University of Washington in Seattle.

Married with three grown children, she and her husband now live in a secluded valley of the Tehachapi Mountains.

Joan Francis

Phone/fax: 661 821-1856

Email: DianaHunterPI@aol.com

Website: www.joanfrancis.net

OTHER BOOKS BY JOAN FRANCIS

  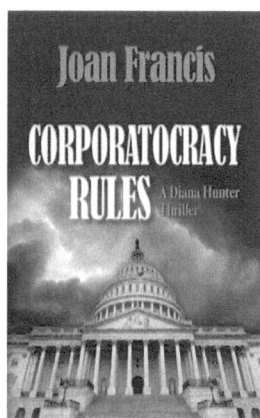

Find paperbacks at Amazon.com and Createspace.com

Find ebooks on Amazon.com, Barnes & Noble.com, Smashwords.com, Apple.com, Sony.com, Kobo.com and Diesel.com.

www.ingramcontent.com/pod-product-compliance
Lightning Source LLC
Chambersburg PA
CBHW020451130626
46549CB00001B/381